Terror at Dark Harbor

***Other Five Star Titles
by Clarissa Ross:***

Mists of Dark Harbor
A Hearse for Dark Harbor
Ghost of Dark Harbor
Secret of the Pale Lover
Dark Harbor Haunting

Clarissa Ross

Terror at Dark Harbor

Five Star
Unity, Maine

Copyright © 1975 by Clarissa Ross

All rights reserved.

Five Star Romance Series.
Published in 2001 in conjunction with the
Maureen Moran Agency.

The text of this edition is unabridged.

Set in 11 pt. Plantin by Al Chase.

Printed in the United States on permanent paper.
Library of Congress Cataloging-in-Publication Data
Ross, Clarissa, 1912–
   Terror at Dark Harbor / Clarissa Ross.
     p. cm. — (Dark Harbor series ; bk. 5)
   ISBN 0-7862-2950-0 (hc : alk. paper)
   I. Title.
PR9199.3.R5996 T47 2001
813'.54—dc21   00-062266

*To Judy and Joe Auerbach
of Boston and Brewster,
who aren't all that far away
from the folks at Dark Harbor!*

CHAPTER ONE

Until that hot July of 1973 when Kim Rice journeyed to Dark Harbor to spend the summer with Johnny Craig and his family, she had never had any reason to believe in ghosts. But not long after she arrived at the fine old brick mansion atop a cliff overlooking the harbor, a ghost appeared to threaten her and change the pattern of her life!

Out of those long, languorous summer days and sometimes thickly fogged nights were to come experiences such as she had never dreamed of, happenings too macabre for her mind to conjure and terror of a sort unknown to her until she came as a summer guest to this tiny island off Cape Cod surrounded by the waters of the Atlantic Ocean.

The web of evil and the supernatural in which she found herself entangled was woven from soft murmurs of conversation in deck chairs under the blazing sun and from eerie whispers which came to her in the cool darkness of a seemingly deserted garden with the scent of wild roses and sweltering pine trees filling the midnight air.

Here amid the rugged beauty of Pirate Island and its town of Dark Harbor, she found herself an actress in a drama more macabre than any in which she had ever appeared on the stage. Confusion and fear became her companions, so that when she at last was confronted by a pale and lovely ghost in a chic dress of shimmering, black sequins dripping from the ocean depths from which she had ascended, she was ready to believe that there were such restless souls who returned from the beyond.

Returned to offer some message which delivered would set their unhappy spirits at rest, or, as in the case of this lovely, wayward phantom, to seek some revenge which life had denied her and which must be satisfied.

But Kim knew nothing of this when she left New York in May to join the Henry Street Playhouse Company in Boston. She was a petite, auburn-haired young woman of twenty-three with greater than average acting ability. This combined with an attractive figure and a pertly pretty face whose chief features were broad cheeks, bright green eyes, and a hint of a snub nose had taken her as far as professional theater in New York City without any important break.

One of the smaller talent agencies had taken her on as a client but had only been able to get her roles Off-Broadway or in the still smaller, though often excellent, Off-Off-Broadway theaters.

As the sophisticated young woman who ran the agency told her, "Kim, darling, this town is full of talented kids like you who have fled the College Dramatic Club in Wisconsin to make a name on Broadway! It just doesn't happen that easy!"

Kim had listened and understood. She was from Wisconsin and she had been active in the college dramatic group there. In fact, she had been the star of the group. Everyone had insisted it would be a crime if she didn't go to New York and give herself the chance she deserved.

Only her widowed mother had been skeptical. When the matter of going to New York had been discussed, her still-attractive mother had warned her, "I can't help you as I'd like. Even being private secretary to the town's leading lawyer doesn't pay me all that much. I will send you what I can. But from all I know, New York is both expensive and cruel. Do you want to risk it?"

"I must, Mother," she'd said with a brave smile. "I'll find

part-time jobs outside the theater and at least give acting a try."

So she had arrived in New York. She lived in a hotel for women for a short while and then took a tiny apartment in Greenwich Village with another aspiring young actress with the unlikely name of Connie Conway. It was a cold-water walk-up, but it served as a headquarters and they managed very well.

Kim found part-time work as a clerk at Gimbel's Department Store and the rest of the week made the rounds looking for work. Her first job was with a tiny company in a converted store in MacDougal Street. A young director noticed her in this part and hired her for his Off-Broadway company. She joined Actor's Equity, the professional union of actors.

Within six months she was playing important parts for the Lolly Theater, an Off-Broadway group uptown on Lexington Avenue doing a repertory season of mystery plays to excellent reviews. Though the upstairs theater was small it had charm, and Kim was happy to be a member of the company.

The advent of summer meant that they would be closing down. She had agreed to return in the first mystery play of the second season for which rehearsals would begin in late September, but until then she had no show business work. The prospect of slaving in Gimbel's for three days and sweltering in her tiny apartment the balance of the time was not appealing.

Then her agent had called her into the office and with her usual blunt acerbity had said, "You'll never get a dramatic job in town this summer, and most of the summer stock work is already cast. But I can get you an interim job for May in Boston. The Henry Street Playhouse is doing a revival of *Night Must Fall*. You've done it here. I submitted your name and they'll take you if you want the job."

"How long will it run?" she'd asked. If the playing time scheduled was too short, it wouldn't be worthwhile moving to Boston and paying for a place to live there since she'd already promised to pay her share of the flat in New York right through the summer. It was the only way she and Connie could afford to keep even such a modest place.

Her agent said, "The play is to run six weeks, almost to the end of June. And they might even extend it a week if it goes well."

"I'll take it," she said promptly.

Her agent was pleased. "I agree that you should. And who knows? Some late opening in one of the summer stock companies may turn up by then. I'll push you for the first opportunity which comes along."

Kim thanked her agent and then went back to the apartment and broke the news to Connie. Blonde, droll Connie was not all that enthused. "Will you really clear so much on the engagement? You'll be paying double living expenses!"

"But I'll be acting," Kim told her with a smile. "And that means a lot to me. I can't stand the prospect of being idle all summer."

Connie sighed. "I suppose you're right, but I'll miss you."

She laughed. "You think that! But I know you! Before I've been gone a day, you'll be having some of the crowd in for a party. You'll do all right!"

The blonde Connie whose long face and droll manner added to her talents as a comic had broken into a shy grin and admitted, "I haven't any gift for being lonely."

So Kim went to Boston. She found the company young and enthusiastic and was able to locate a studio apartment on Huntington Avenue which she could sublet. The director of the Emlyn Williams play was a young man she'd known in New York and the stage manager, Bill Griffith, was also a friend who had played with the Lolly Players once. He was a jovial, sandy-haired young man who liked the supervisory work of stage manager better than acting. He set about making her at home in Boston and telling her all about the company she'd be working with for the next nine weeks or so.

They were sitting at a window table in a coffee shop not far from the theater on the evening after the first rehearsal. The actor playing the part of Dan, the hotel-steward murderer who carries around a girl's severed head in a leather box, had not arrived. So Bill Griffith had filled in this important lead role for the rehearsal.

A candle burned in a bottle on the table between them. There was a steady murmur of conversation in the well-filled place so that in the near-dark atmosphere one had a deceptive feeling of privacy. The coffee shop was a favorite meeting place for the actors and other young people of the downtown Boston area.

She asked Bill, "When does the actor playing Dan arrive? Or will you be doing the part?"

Bill's boyish, rather thin face showed a smile. "No chance of my doing it. The theater is going to feature Johnny Craig in the role. They've got all the advertising ready for a big splurge!"

She was excited by the information. "Johnny Craig! He's the one who just had such rave reviews in that movie about motorcyclists, isn't he?"

Bill took a sip of his coffee. He asked her, "Have you seen the film?"

"Yes. Everyone in New York was talking about it."

He nodded. "Even though it's just a quickie production! It won't make the big chains because it was too cheaply made. But it sure corraled some neat reviews and raves for Johnny's performance."

Kim smiled. "I read a short article on him in the *New York Post*. They called him the playboy leading man. He's very wealthy, isn't he?"

"Wealthy and old family as well," Bill Griffith said, his boyish face highlighted by the glow of the candle. "His ancestors lived on an island off the coast of Cape Cod—Pirate Island. They had whaling ships and made a fortune in whale oil in the days when it was in great demand."

"And the family has continued to be wealthy through the years?"

"Yes. A lot of the old whaling families lost their fortunes when whaling went out of vogue. But not the Craig clan. They went into banking in Boston, and they are richer than ever now."

"Interesting," she said.

"They still go to Pirate Island for the summer," Bill went on. "They have a picturesque old mansion built by Johnny's great-grandfather which sits on a cliff just outside the island's largest town, Dark Harbor."

"I'm sure there was some mention of it in the article," she said with a slight frown as she tried to recall this.

"No doubt," Bill said. "In any case, it is a favorite spot of Johnny's. I understand he's down there now, but he'll be coming up to join us for rehearsals tomorrow."

"Is he serious about his acting?" she asked.

Bill shrugged. "Not like you and I. But he probably does have as much interest in an acting career as in anything else. The story is that he bankrolled that film with the understanding he'd be the star. It was a smart move. It made his name."

"But he'd done other things before that?"

"Lots of things," Bill said. "He's older than we are. Must be in his mid-thirties."

Kim was surprised. "He looks younger than that."

"Lots of youthful charm," Bill said grimly. "You'll be exposed to it tomorrow. Don't be taken in by it."

Her eyebrows raised. "Now what does that mean?"

"Just what I say," Bill Griffith said looking at her very directly. "You'll be meeting him tomorrow. Watch out!"

Confused, she said, "You make him sound like some sort of ogre! Please explain!"

Bill hesitated. "I don't want to be unfair to him."

"Go on!" she urged.

He sighed. "Let's say his record isn't good."

"In what way?"

"In all ways," Bill told her. "I guess it comes from having too much money. He studied theater in London after he was thrown out of college here. A real scandal at the time! A girl fell or jumped from the window of a sorority house during a party."

"They didn't mention that in the article I read."

"Not likely," he said with a thin smile. "Johnny has a lot of influence. That helps him get a good press. When he came back to this country, be managed to get a Broadway part which brought him good notices. I don't say he hasn't talent, but his money bought him the breaks."

"I see," she said, not too surprised. She'd heard stories like this before.

"He went from one show to another with long idle spells between," Bill said. "He also did some television and movie work. And most of the time he managed to get favorable mention of his work. But his personal habits have been another matter. They don't get him such good reports."

"Oh?"

"He has a habit of dropping out of shows in mid-run and leaving the management to substitute an understudy or whoever they can get. I think the people here are taking a chance on him in this show. He is also reported to come drunk to the theater too often."

"That's bad."

"Real bad!" Bill agreed with a sigh. "And then there are things that are whispered about but which can't be proven."

She stared across the candle flame at him. "What sort of things?"

Bill said, "Not what you enjoy discussing. They say he's a little mad. A kind of sadist. He's never married although he's been engaged a half-dozen times. The things that happened to some of those girls is kind of upsetting."

Kim was startled by the grim tone of the young man as he spoke about Johnny Craig. She asked, "What has happened? It's all news to me."

Again the young man hesitated. "I don't want you to think I'm jealous of him or trying to turn you against him even before you meet him."

"I don't think that. I know you're always fair to people," she said.

"I try to be."

"I accept that," she said almost impatiently. "Please go on and tell me what this Johnny Craig has done."

He stared down at his empty coffee cup. "One girl's face was all battered after they had a quarrel. She accused Johnny at first and then withdrew the charges."

"It was in the papers?"

"Sure. Photos and all. About five years ago."

She grimaced. "I was back in Wisconsin then. I wouldn't have been interested."

He smiled. "Too busy with the college drama group."

"Something like that."

"Then there were other cases where girls claimed he'd set

out to deliberately hurt them. Once in a hotel in Washington he was supposed to have made a tureen of scalding hot soup spill over a girl's shoulder and breast. He claimed he'd done it inadvertently because he'd been drinking too much. The girl said it was no accident. Somehow it was settled."

"He sounds vicious," she said in an awed tone.

"That isn't the end of it," Bill assured her. "One night in New York his girlfriend at the time fell or was pushed out of the front seat of the car he was driving. You can choose your version. He said she fell because the door wasn't properly shut and she claimed he had deliberately shoved her over and out."

"Who do you think was telling the truth?"

"In view of those other things, my bet is on the girl," Bill said. "The girl was in hospital for months and was left with a bad leg from a permanent back injury. The settlement for that cost him plenty."

She could not understand why, but she found herself asking, "How can you be so sure Johnny Craig was to blame in all these instances? Couldn't some of these girls have lied to sue him? Rich young men are often targets for unscrupulous young women."

Bill registered amazement. "You sound exactly like his attorneys. That's the line they've always used to get him out of trouble."

She smiled in embarrassment. "I didn't mean to sound silly, but isn't it a possibility that in many of these cases he has been wronged rather than doing wrong? Once a rich playboy has been tagged with a bad name, you can have him blamed for almost anything."

He stared at her with a wry smile. "I swear Johnny's charm must exude from the screen and hypnotize people. Here you are defending him, and you haven't even met him."

Kim blushed. "I'm only trying to be fair. I do have to do a

lot of scenes with him in this play. I don't want a hostile attitude on my part to show—especially if it isn't justified."

Bill said, "Maybe I shouldn't have told you about him. I've tried to be honest. I thought I should let you understand the sort of man he is."

"I appreciate that."

"You could be right," Bill admitted with a sigh. "All those young women could have been out to shake him down for money. If so, his lawyers played into their hands. They've always settled for him."

"I know it's hard to be sure," she said in a troubled tone. "But people always seem to suspect the wealthy of the worst. You will admit this Johnny Craig could be a victim of the wrong sort of girl."

Bill said, "I'll willingly admit it, though I have my doubts. But you decide when you meet Johnny tomorrow. He has promised to leave Pirate Island and be up here in time for rehearsal."

A feeling of excitement rippled through Kim again as she told Bill, "I'm looking forward to the meeting. I'll tell you what I think of him."

The next morning would have offered only a routine rehearsal but for the expected arrival of the star, Johnny Craig. Kim sat in one of the front rows of the theater-in-the-round Henry Street Playhouse as the director coached the character woman and one of the other actors in a scene. He was making the best use of his time as he waited for Johnny to show up.

Suddenly there was an air of expectation in the shadowed auditorium as a tall, lithe young man in a colorful sport shirt open at the neck and white slacks came marching down one of the aisles to the stage. Kim had lifted her eyes from her script to study the newcomer and saw the familiar, good-humored, square-jawed face, shrewd blue eyes and corn-blond hair of the well-known playboy and actor.

He saw Kim and offered her a warm smile. "Hello," he said. "I'm glad you're one of the company."

From the stage Tony Parker, the dark, lantern-jawed director reached down to shake hands with Johnny. "Hi," the director said. "I've been filling in while we waited for you."

Johnny shook hands and said, "Traffic was heavy coming in from the airport. The flight up took no time, but then we got snarled up coming into the city."

"I thought you might be driving," the director said.

"Not a chance. That would have meant getting the early ferry and a long drive up from Hyannis. Flying was the ideal solution."

Tony nodded. "We'll get under way at once. I'll introduce you to the company so we can begin."

When it came time for Kim to be introduced to the star he had a special smile for her. He said, "I'm sure I've seen you in New York. Weren't you working at the Lolly Playhouse?"

It came as a surprise to her that he should recognize her. Somewhat flustered, she said, "Yes. Do you really remember me?"

"Of course," Johnny Craig said. "I went there one night with some friends. I intended to go backstage, but instead we went down to the restaurant below. You were in the Agatha Christie play. I wanted to congratulate you."

Kim was delighted. "Thank you."

"I think you'll be exactly right for this also," he said before he moved on to meet the character woman.

Bill Griffith was standing nearby during the introductions and had overheard the exchange. Now there was a dolefully humorous look on his boyish face. His expression clearly said, *I warned you, but I never did expect you to be able to resist him!*

Kim made up her mind to be especially reserved towards the handsome star. She even questioned that he was going to be good in the role of the young Cockney murderer. Johnny, with his dashing good looks and cultured Yankee accent, hardly seemed right. But when he took his script in hand and began to read the lines, she was impressed. His Cockney accent was amazingly authentic, and then she recalled that he had studied drama in London so would be able to handle most British accents well. His swagger as the conceited killer was just right, and she soon felt that once again he would turn in a fine performance. When she played her scenes with him, she found the experience completely satisfying.

When the rehearsal ended, Johnny Craig and the director left the auditorium together in earnest conversation. Kim picked up her sweater and a script and was about to go also when Bill Griffith nimbly jumped down from the stage to join her.

He gave her a knowing smile and said, "How about taking a stroll on the Common? It's a lovely day and I can use some air after working in here all morning."

Kim returned his smile. "Why not?"

It was not until they left the theater and the others who were associated with the production behind that they began to talk. They crossed the several blocks until they reached Boylston Street and beyond it the large Boston park known as the Common. The sun was warm, many of the park benches were filled, and dogs of all shapes and sizes ran without benefit of leash giving the nimble gray squirrels a bad time. When dogs came close, the squirrels would scamper up one of the many ancient trees which decorated the Common.

Feeling greatly relaxed, Kim said, "I think I'm going to like Boston in spite of the awful apartment I'm living in."

Bill nodded. "It's a nice old city. But I'm not interested in your opinion of Boston. I'd much rather hear what you think of Johnny Craig."

They were walking hand in hand and now she turned to look up at him with an amused smile on her pert face. She said, "I was sure you'd get around to that."

"How could I help it?" he asked. "I saw your shy schoolgirl act when he talked to you. I was afraid you'd pull a Victorian swoon for his benefit."

"Stop it!" she protested.

"I mean it," he said. "You did look bowled over."

"He was so nice!" Kim protested.

"I warned you he would be."

"You warned me about a lot of things!"

"You haven't answered me yet," Bill reminded her as they kept strolling.

She watched several pigeons waddle off and take flight as she considered what she'd say. Then she told the young stage manager, "I think you must be wrong about him. He's thoughtful and nice, and above all else, he's an excellent actor."

"So you're completely sold on him?"

"I'm afraid I am," she said.

"It worries me, too," Bill said sincerely. "I hate to think of your being let down, and I have the odd feeling you will be before this show is over."

She gave him a reproachful glance. "Don't be such a harbinger of gloom! And don't think I'm serious about Johnny Craig. I happen to like him and that's that. He's just another member of the company as far as I'm concerned. I'm going to be careful not to become personally involved with him."

Bill Griffith brightened. "I hope you mean that."

"I do."

"Then I'll have less cause to worry about you," he said. "Just remember that. No personal involvements. It's apt to save you a lot of pain."

"Thanks," she said, a little acidly. She felt he was making far too much of the star's shortcomings. And she honestly meant to keep her relationship with Johnny on a strictly professional level. She didn't know then that the charming Johnny had made up his mind to change that.

Nor did she find out for quite some time. Meanwhile the rehearsals for *Night Must Fall* continued in an excellent fashion. Kim felt sure the play would be well received as a revival and that it would run its full engagement in Boston. Director Tony Parker seemed to be of the same opinion; in fact, no one was worried about the show's success.

Then, the night before the dress rehearsal, Johnny didn't appear on time. And when he arrived more than an hour late he had liquor on his breath and showed signs of being drunk. Director Tony Parker took it in his stride. Bill Griffith had been filling in for the part, and he at once gave the stage to Johnny. The rehearsal continued tensely. In her scenes with Johnny, Kim learned unpleasantly that his drunken state threw off all the timing they'd worked out earlier.

Tony said nothing when the rehearsal was over. He merely asked everyone to be on time for dress rehearsal and then stepped down from the stage and stalked out of the auditorium without offering a word to Johnny. This was noticeable because the two were always talking.

Johnny turned to Kim and in a slightly, slurred voice said, "I guess I'm in the doghouse tonight."

She quietly said, "Don't you think you deserve to be? You ruined the rehearsal."

"I'll be great tomorrow and when we open," was his promise.

"I hope so," she said. "I need the work. I want this play to have its full run."

"Don't worry," he told her. And then he added, "I'm going to the lounge at the Ritz-Carlton Hotel to have lunch and get sobered up. Come along to make sure I don't start drinking again. It's sort of nice. They have a pianist up there."

Normally she would have turned him down, since she'd made up her mind to avoid a personal friendship with him. But there was something so pathetic in the way he gave the invitation that she found it difficult to refuse him. And though she usually had coffee with Bill Griffith after the show, she decided it might be best all around to try and keep the star on the straight and narrow.

"All right," she said. "I wouldn't mind a before midnight snack. But I don't want anything but coffee to drink."

"That's the idea," Johnny promised her. "The only reason I plan to go to the lounge is that it's the one place in the hotel which serves food at this time of night."

He escorted her outside and hailed the first passing taxi. Just as they settled down in it for the ride to the Ritz-Carlton, she saw Bill come out on the street in search of her. When he saw her in the car with Johnny, his youthful face dropped and he turned away to head down the street. She felt as if she'd taken part in a betrayal and at the same time tried to reassure herself by reasoning that she was being nice to the star for the good of all the company.

Johnny turned to smile at her in the taxi. "I'm surprised you agreed to go out with me," he confessed. "All along I've had a feeling you were avoiding me."

"I can't think why," she said evasively.

He chuckled. "Could it be our callow young stage manager who holds the key to your heart?"

She blushed. "Bill Griffith and I are good friends."

"I saw that," the star said. He reached out and took her hand in his. "I want us to be good friends as well."

She made no reply and freed her hand from his as soon as she could manage it without seeming offensive. They reached the staid old hotel and he saw her upstairs to the second-floor lounge, which was almost deserted. A pianist held forth at a grand piano, playing in a subdued mood. They were greeted by a mature headwaiter who saw them to a table opposite the piano and took their double orders for sausage, home-fried potatoes and scrambled eggs.

"I shouldn't eat so much so late," she protested, laughing.

Johnny Craig was in good humor. "Wash it down with coffee and you'll never notice it," he advised her. "I wonder we haven't gotten around to this before."

"We've been busy," she said, not wanting to discuss this.

"And you've always managed to avoid me except when we are onstage," he pointed out, the shrewd blue eyes fixed on her.

She shrugged. "I hadn't meant to."

"Still you have," he persisted. "Why? Have people been telling you stories about me? Or have you been reading the gossip newspapers and magazines?"

"Maybe a little of both," she confessed.

Johnny frowned. "I know those papers make me sound like a nasty character. Don't believe what they say."

"All right," she said. "And please don't drink anymore when you're at the theater. It kills morale. And you're so good in the play everyone is counting on you."

"You, too?"

"Especially. I need this play to be a success."

"It's going to be," he said. He seemed much more sober than he had been even before getting the food and coffee they'd ordered.

The pianist began playing a popular romantic tune as they waited for their orders. She said, "I hope they aren't going to be too long. I have to take the subway home and I don't want to be too late."

Johnny shook his head in good-humored disgust. "Take a subway home? Not while you're my date!"

"I'm used to taking the subway," she said.

"You won't take it tonight," the star promised. "I shall see you to your door."

"There's no need," she protested. "You can head to wherever your hotel room is after we part."

"My hotel room is here," the blond young man said. "This is where I stay in Boston."

"Oh?" she said.

"So I'm home right now," he told her with a drunken chuckle. "I like the way you're trying to mother me. It's a good sign and I won't forget it."

Even more flustered, she said, "I want to be your friend. We are working together."

"Sure we are," he said. "One of the reasons I've stayed with the show is that you are in it."

Kim was startled. "You didn't think of leaving us during rehearsals?"

"Why not?" he asked. "I've done it before."

She gave him a look of reproof. "I don't much admire quitters."

"I'll remember that," he told her jeeringly. The situation was saved by the arrival of the food. It was good and she enjoyed it. He also seemed happy with the midnight lunch.

The waiter poured their coffee and then moved a discreet distance away once again. It was clear that the hotel staff were used to catering to the millionaire playboy.

More sober now he sipped his coffee and then said, "I

want you to get to really know me as a person."

She smiled nervously. "I think I know you."

"You don't," the young man said, his voice sharp suddenly. "All that stuff in the newspapers is lies. They picture me as a decadent playboy. That's nowhere near the truth. You should see me living the simple life at Dark Harbor."

"You enjoy your island retreat?"

"My favorite place," he said. "Built by an ancestor of mine. We made our money there in whaling days. My family all go there for the summer. I even have a girl there whom I'm extremely fond of."

"Oh?" This was interesting.

"I think she might be willing to marry me," the star said carelessly. "I'm not certain, mind you. But the possibility is there."

"What about you?"

"I like her, but I can't make up my mind," he said. "I'm not all that anxious to be married. All my engagements to date have turned out to be disasters."

"You probably haven't met the right girl," she suggested.

"I agree," the star said. "And what is more, I'll know when I meet the right one."

"I'm sure you will," she said.

His eyes were fixed on her in a sort of strange way as he told her, "You know, you're lovely. An extremely pretty girl."

"Thank you, but you're flattering me," she said. "I'm no beauty and I know it."

"I mean what I said," he assured her almost harshly, and then asked, "Will you have some more coffee?"

"Just a little," she told him, and she held out her cup for him to fill.

With a sudden, peculiar smile he picked up the silver coffeepot and held it poised above her cup. Then—quite unexpectedly—he tilted the spout of the silver decanter just a trifle so that the stream of boiling hot coffee painfully flowed over her hand. She cried out and let the cup fall!

CHAPTER TWO

There was instant pandemonium in the Ritz-Carlton's staid lounge. The waiter came rushing to assist Kim while Johnny Craig put the silver pot aside with an oath. Then the headwaiter came with a bucket of ice and assisted her in applying it to the scalded area of her hand. The ice eased the pain and she began to regain some poise.

"It's not really bad at all," she protested, aware that the half-dozen other patrons in the place were taking in the spectacle with suitably polite horror.

Johnny stood over her with his face in shadow. "What a fool I am!" he exclaimed. "I should have waited for the waiter to pour your coffee! I felt it change weight in my hands as the fluid moved. I'm terribly awkward in such things!"

She glanced up at him. "It's scalded only lightly. It feels much better now. It will be all right."

The headwaiter was troubled. "You should see a doctor, Miss. Go to one of the emergency outpatient departments. They'll take care of this properly."

She demurred. "I don't think such a fuss need be made about it."

Johnny frowned. "The waiter is right. We don't want any kind of complications. I'll get a taxi and take you to the nearest emergency room."

One of the elderly men who had been standing in the background now came forward and said, "Please forgive my intruding. I'm a doctor and I have an office on Arlington Street only a few doors from here. If the young lady will go there, I'll take care of her hand."

Kim managed a wan smile for him. "You're too kind. There is no need to bother you if there is a hospital emergency room close by."

The veteran doctor showed grim amusement on his thin face. "There are emergency departments open and available to you, but I don't think you have any kind of a picture of them. Most of them are crowded at this time of night and the cases waiting for aid aren't all that pleasant. You get drunks, stab wounds, and the like. I wouldn't send my wife or daughter to one if I could avoid it. That is why I'm making you this offer."

Johnny Craig spoke up, "We'll accept, doctor."

"Dr. Vernon Meadows," the thin man said. "My office is in the building at Eight Arlington Street. I'll go there now and be ready when you arrive."

"Thank you so much, Dr. Meadows," Kim said gratefully.

"Not at all," the elderly doctor said. "I'm used to this sort of thing. Part of my profession." And he left them and went across to notify his male companion of his decision before exiting from the lounge.

The headwaiter told her in a low voice, "He is one of Boston's best surgeons. You need not worry about him."

"I'm sure he's competent," she agreed. "And thank you for the ice. It's helped a lot—I don't think my hand will blister much."

Johnny had sat down again and he stared across at her bleakly. "I don't dare think what Tony Parker will say about this. I could have scalded you badly enough to put you out of the play."

"You didn't, so let's not dwell on that," she said.

"Feel better?" he asked.

"Yes," she said. Now that the pain had subsided and the

general commotion was at an end, she was beginning to review the incident in her mind.

What upset her was the impression she had that Johnny had deliberately swayed the spout of the silver coffeepot to pour the scalding liquid on her hand. He claimed that he was awkward at pouring and the shifting weight of the liquid had caused him to make the error. But she was not all that sure.

She remembered the strange way Bill Griffith had spoken about the young star. He had suggested that Johnny Craig was a confirmed sadist who enjoyed inflicting pain on people. And his particular enjoyment seemed in the past to have been concentrated on making young women infatuated with him suffer in various ways. Could the monstrous rumors about him be true? Was he a trifle mad in this connection?

He gave her an uneasy look. "What is it?" he asked. "You seem lost in thought."

"Sorry," she said. "I guess I'm still in shock."

He glanced across the room. "The doctor has been gone quite a few minutes. We'd better follow him to his office. We don't want to keep him waiting."

She glanced at her hand. "It's not bad at all. I feel it is wrong to bother him."

"Nonsense," her escort said. "He's offered to look after you. And I'll feel better to know that a doctor has taken care of it."

Kim sighed. "Very well," she said. "Let's get it over with. I still have quite a long way to go to my apartment, and we have an early rehearsal tomorrow."

Johnny paid their check and they left the now deserted lounge. They went downstairs and walked across the Commonwealth Avenue intersection to the imposing stone building on Arlington Street in which the doctor's office was located. The doctor's friend was waiting in the vestibule for them.

The man explained, "I have a key. At this time of night there is no doorman to let you in. This will save Dr. Meadows from coming down."

"You're both extremely kind," Kim said as the man unlocked the door and led them across the small lobby to a self-service elevator. They took the elevator up to the third floor, Johnny all the while seeming tense and unhappy.

Dr. Meadows greeted them when they stepped out of the elevator. He had his friend and Johnny wait in the outer office while he took Kim into his examining room. Under the bright light available there, he examined the burn and put a healing ointment on it.

He said, "It's not too bad. It will probably peel and may feel stiff and painful for a few days. I'll give you a tube of this ointment to apply."

"I feel I was so lucky you were there," she said.

The old doctor brought her the tube of ointment and handed it to her as he studied her with a searching look. "How well do you know that young man?" he asked.

She shrugged. "He's a friend. A new friend. I've only just met him."

Dr. Meadows frowned. "I don't want to upset you, but I saw all that happened. It seems to me the accident was avoidable. That young man was needlessly careless."

Kim tried to hide her upset. It was startling to have the elderly doctor confirm what she had already decided. It was more than that, it was somewhat terrifying. Trying to keep her tone light, she said, "Johnny feels more concerned about it than I do."

"You heard what I said just now," the thin man said staring at her hard.

She nodded uneasily. "Yes. But it's over with now. No need for recriminations. They seldom do any good."

"I agree," Dr. Meadows said grimly. "But I want you to know what my impression of the accident was. If you continue your friendship with this young man, you could be exposing yourself to other accidents."

She said, "You mean you think he's accident-prone?"

"Something like that."

"I promise I'll keep that in mind," she told him.

He was very serious as he said, "I hope that you will. That was my main reason for having you here. To tell you. I would try and avoid future contacts with that young man if I were you."

She smiled wryly. "I'm afraid that won't be too easy. You see we are both acting in a play that is opening soon at the Henry Street Theater."

Dr. Meadows looked surprised and concerned. "That does place a different aspect on things."

"Yes. We're bound to see a lot of each other both in and out of the theater."

"I can only repeat; be careful of him."

She said, "I will. Though you could be wrong. The accident might have been simply that. I doubt that it was intended."

Dr. Meadows sighed. "I hope not. Take care of your hand and best of luck with the play!"

They left the doctor's office and Johnny hailed another taxi and gave the driver her Huntington Avenue address. Then they sat back in the dark interior of the cab to take the journey in ease.

Johnny said, "I hope that doctor was helpful. He behaved rather coolly towards me."

"He's a good doctor," she said, glancing at her companion in the shadows. "And I think you imagined that business of his being cool to you." She knew that he had been, but did not want to discuss it with Johnny at this time.

Johnny was insistent. He went on, "I say he was cool. He acted as if I were to blame for what happened—as if it hadn't been an accident."

"Even if you were clumsy, he couldn't very well blame you," she said.

"Maybe not," the young man beside her said ruefully, "but I got the impression he didn't like me. I can tell with people."

"Don't think about it," she said.

He gazed at her in the near darkness. "You forgive me for what happened, don't you?"

"Of course," she said, trying to show no emotion.

"You're sure?"

"Sure," she said. "Let's not talk about it anymore. I want to try and forget it happened."

"Small chance," he said almost jeeringly. "That hand won't be all that comfortable for a few days. You're bound to find it painful."

"I can stand the pain," she said, "as long as we don't keep on discussing it." She was uneasily aware that he wanted to talk about it, as if dwelling on it gave him a secret pleasure.

They reached her apartment building in about twenty minutes. Johnny left the taxi with her and saw her safely inside. He was almost boyishly concerned as he said good night.

"I'll not soon forgive myself for what happened," he told her.

She managed a small parting smile for him. "We won't even talk about it again."

His eyes showed admiration as he said in a low voice, "You're a brave, lovely girl." And he gave her a warm good-night kiss. "See you at the theater in the morning." Then he left her.

She went into her tiny apartment filled with confusion. In one sense, he'd been a gallant, tender escort, and yet in another he'd been a good deal less. In her final summing up of it all, she decided that it had been an accident and Johnny hadn't been to blame. In spite of what the doctor had said, she refused to believe there was anything sinister about what had happened.

So she went to bed and slept as well as her troublesome hand allowed. In the morning she treated it with the ointment, but knew it was going to be painful for a week or so. She hoped that by the time the play opened all signs of the burn would have vanished. There might be a small scar left, but she could easily cover it with makeup.

Keeping her word, she said nothing about it at rehearsal the next morning. Tony Parker was so busy putting the cast through their paces that he didn't notice it and not until the rehearsal ended and she strolled out into the street in the company of Bill Griffith did anyone see that her hand had been injured.

Bill stared at the scald and whistled. "How did that happen?"

She told him, and with a knowing glance added, "Don't jump to any rash conclusions."

Bill said, "I guess you know what I'm thinking."

"Johnny didn't do it deliberately."

"How can you be sure?" he asked her.

"I was the victim. I know how it happened."

"I wonder," Bill worried. "I warned you there is a queer cruel streak in Johnny."

"You made so much of it I find I'm a little afraid of him," she protested.

"It seems it would be wise for you to remain afraid," was Bill's reply.

"No," she said. "That's not being fair to Johnny. It's over. Let's forget about it."

Bill Griffith gave her a skeptical look. "I only hope you'll be as broad-minded if I decide to treat you in the same way."

She smiled at him. "I'm not worried about you!"

Bill raised his eyes to heaven. "That's my misfortune. Women refuse to take me seriously!"

The friendship they had was a good one. And as the days and nights of preparing *Night Must Fall* went by, they came to know each other even better. The play was going well and an elderly actress, Babs Darriot, who was playing the part originated by Dame May Whitty, was excellent. As the petulant, opinionated old woman who was eventually to be murdered by the pageboy she'd befriended, she was giving a star performance.

Johnny Craig seemed to resent the impact she was making in the role. He once told Kim in a low aside, "That greedy old girl is trying to steal the show from the rest of us!"

Kim had shown amusement at this. "But that's the idea, Johnny. The better she is, the more she'll build up your part. A play like this depends on teamwork. When one member of the cast is strong like Babs Darriot, it builds up all of us."

"You think so?" he sounded doubtful.

"I'm certain of it," she had said. "It would be different if she stood out above everyone else. But none of us are giving weak performances, so it is fine to have her give the part lots of strength."

"Maybe you're right," Johnny said, but she could tell by his tone that he wasn't convinced.

Opening night should have satisfied him. The house was filled with the usual first-night audience of critics, friends of the producers and cast, and the theater buffs who liked to be first to see any new offering. For an opening-night audience they were rapt in their attention and generous in their applause.

When the final curtain came down and rose again for Kim to take a number of bows along with Johnny and Babs Darriot, there could be no question that they had a hit on their hands. A party had been scheduled at the restaurant next door to the theater and Kim hastened upstairs to the dressing room which was next to that of Babs Darriot.

The buxom character woman, still in her gray wig and black dress, paused at the top of the backstage landing, gasping for breath from the exertion of hurrying up the stairs, as she told Kim, "I think they really liked us!"

"I know they did," Kim agreed. "You were great and so was Johnny."

"And you were exactly right for the play," the character woman told her graciously. "All the cast are good. I'm glad to be working again. It has been a poor year for me."

Kim smiled at the older woman. "We'll get the full six weeks promised and likely the extra one as well."

"I do hope so," the elderly character actress said worriedly. "You never can tell with Johnny Craig. If he takes it in his head, he'll walk off anytime and leave the company to fold."

"Surely he wouldn't do that!" she protested.

"It has happened before," the old actress warned her and then hobbled on to her dressing room and went inside.

Kim quickly changed from her stage clothes and makeup to an outfit suitable for the party. Then she went downstairs in search of Bill Griffith. Since the night when she'd had the misadventure at Johnny's hands, she had avoided the star except when they were onstage together. If Johnny noticed this, he didn't say anything about it. She hoped that the work and rush of rehearsals had made it seem more as if she were merely too busy to see him.

Bill came out from backstage to join her in the deserted auditorium. He said, "It's a great show."

"Thanks," she said with a smile.

"How is the hand?"

"As good as new," she said.

"I'm still suspicious of Johnny Craig," the stage manager said as they started out of the theater for the restaurant next door and the party going on there.

By the time they entered the restaurant, music was playing and a good-sized crowd were enjoying themselves in boisterous fashion. Johnny came over to greet her with his handsome face flushed and a drink in his hand. The star told her, "Most of my family is up from Cape Cod to see the opening. I want you to meet them. They're looking forward to meeting you."

She said, "Really? I'd imagine they'd be much more interested in Babs Darriot. Next to you, she is the star of the show."

Johnny said, "They want to meet you. Come along!" And without giving her any chance to escape he led her by the arm across the restaurant to where a stern, white-haired man and his aristocratic-looking white-haired wife were standing. He introduced her, "Father and Mother, I want you to meet my co-worker, Kim Rice."

Stephen Craig was gracious in a reserved way. He took her hand in a brief, limp grasp and said, "I enjoyed you. In fact, I liked the play better than I expected."

"Thank you," she said, rather shyly.

Madeline Craig, Johnny's mother, was more friendly. In her precise voice she told her, "I saw the movie with

Robert Montgomery in the lead, and I must say I liked Johnny a lot better. Of course I probably am prejudiced."

"I think Johnny is excellent," Kim said, she could see that Madeline Craig was of the same aloof, stern New England breed as her husband. It was a wonder they had produced a son as outgoing as Johnny.

Madeline Craig talked with her while Johnny and his father had some serious discussion. During her conversation with the older woman, a brown-haired girl with a suave-looking man in his thirties came up to join them.

Johnny's mother immediately said, "Miss Rice, you must meet my daughter, Irma, and Jim Blake. She and Jim are engaged."

Irma Craig had an oval, pleasant face which in no way resembled Johnny's square-cut features, but she did have her mother's smile and gracious manner as she extended her hand to Kim and said, "So you are the girl Johnny has talked about so much!"

Kim blushed. "I can't think why. We've only just met."

Irma gave her a reassuring glance. "It doesn't take Johnny long to make up his mind about friends." And she turned to the dark-haired man with a tiny mustache who stood waiting to join in the conversation. "Jim is our family lawyer and he has a place at Dark Harbor not far from us."

"Not a mansion like the Craigs'," Jim said with a thin smile on his thin, intelligent face, "I live in a small cottage, but I do have a view of the ocean."

"That is the most important thing," Kim said.

"Yes," Jim Blake agreed. "Not much point of living on an island if you don't have a house on the shore. You were great in the play."

"Yes," Irma said, giving her an appraising look. "I can now understand why Johnny thinks so much of you. In spite of what people think, he is genuinely dedicated to acting and he appreciates talent."

"I consider him a very good actor," Kim agreed. She had the uneasy feeling that she was being studied and appraised by the pretty brown-haired girl, just as she'd felt the same thing about Johnny's father and mother. She had the impression they were a closely knit family and from long association Jim Blake had come to be regarded as one of them. Yet they would all still regard her as someone very much outside the fold.

Before they could ask her any more questions, Tony Parker, the director, came over, and told her, "I have some people who want to meet you, Kim."

She quickly excused herself from the Craigs and noted that Irma looked disappointed that their conversation should be interrupted so soon. As she strolled away with Tony, Kim said, "Thanks for rescuing me. Johnny's family was giving me a third degree."

Tony showed interest. "I wonder why. Has Johnny shown any deep interest in you?"

"Not that I'm aware of," she said. "I've hardly seen him outside the theater lately."

"You never know with Johnny," the director sighed. And he halted to introduce her to an elderly couple who were supporters of the theater and who had recently met Emlyn Williams in person during one of his many tours doing Dickens readings.

It was not until near the end of the party when most of the guests had left that she and Johnny came face to face again. The star of the play gave her a reproving look and said, "Why did you rush away from my folks?"

"I didn't," she protested. "I talked to them for quite a while until Tony took me away to meet someone else."

Still showing chagrin, Johnny said, "I was getting something settled with my father, and when I turned around you'd gone."

"I did have a nice chat with your sister and her fiancé," she told him.

Johnny's face clouded slightly. "Jim Blake! How did you like him?"

"He seemed very nice," she said.

"He's a climber," Johnny said with disgust in his voice. "But there's no question that Irma will marry him. Jim is the family lawyer, so my folks are resigned to it."

Kim was surprised by the tone in which Johnny discussed his future brother-in-law and only then realized that beneath the young man's liberal facade there was the same snobbish attitude which his father and mother openly showed. Tony was right when he described Johnny as a most complex person.

Johnny asked, "May I see you home?"

"Sorry," she said lightly. "I've already promised Bill I'd let him take me home."

The handsome star scowled. "You've been seeing a lot of him, haven't you?"

"We're friends," she said. "We worked together in New York."

"I know," he said rather absently. "Well, some other time then."

So the opening night passed. The reviews were excellent, but praise for Johnny's performance was at least equaled by plaudits for veteran character actress, Babs Darriot. Everyone in the company was glad for her excellent performance with the possible exception of Johnny. He congratulated Babs, but Kim noticed that he did so with little enthusiasm.

Nothing of note happened for the first three weeks of the run. To placate Johnny, she had lunch with him a couple of times, but she was careful not to encourage him to take any special interest in her. He was more agreeable than he had been before the show opened, and as time went by she forgot all about the incident in which he'd scalded her hand—until something happened one night between the acts to remind her of it all too vividly.

Kim, Johnny, and Babs Darriot were hastening down the steep stairway from the dressing room to backstage. The old actress was in the lead, with Johnny almost directly behind her, and Kim following in third place. Just as they neared the bottom of the tricky steps, she saw Johnny lunge forward and heard the veteran actress cry out!

It took place in a second! As a result, Babs Darriot plunged forward with hands outstretched and a terrified scream on her lips. She fell sprawling on the floor at the bottom of the stairway. Johnny was at her side in a moment, all solicitous.

"Babs!" he said in an upset voice. "Are you hurt? I'm so sorry! I was too close behind you! When I stumbled, I shoved you! Please forgive me!"

The old actress tried sitting up and moaned, "My wrist!"

A concerned Kim was now kneeling beside her. She gave Johnny a reproachful glance as she asked, "Couldn't you have stopped yourself colliding with her?"

He looked confused and miserable. "I was rushing along too close behind her! If she hadn't slowed down, I wouldn't have bumped into her."

Kim wasn't at all certain about this. It could be true, and then again he might have deliberately shoved the old actress out of jealousy. She decided it was too involved a question to settle at the moment. She gave her full attention to the injured woman and asked her, "Is your wrist hurting badly?"

"I can't bear it!" Babs Darriot sobbed. She looked as if she might faint.

Bill Griffith came burning on the scene, demanding, "What has happened?"

Kim glanced up at him. "Babs has had a nasty fall. Her wrist may be broken. Her understudy will have to go on."

And that was how it turned out. The veteran actress had to be rushed to a nearby hospital for treatment. It was found she had broken two ribs in addition to her wrist, and would be out of the play for the balance of the engagement. Not only was it a tragedy for her, it meant that the play suffered. The understudy, a younger woman, was adequate in the role, but no more. The play limped along with attendance dwindling in the final weeks.

Not until a week or so after the accident did Kim dare to talk to Bill Griffith about it. They were having a snack after the show at the coffee shop down the street which the company patronized and were discussing the evening's performance, an uneven one.

Bill sighed. "Since Babs has been out of the show, it has had no balance. Of course Johnny shines, but he needed her playing to make the story believable. The girl who's doing the part now is too obviously acting."

She gave the young man across the candle-lit table from her a solemn look. "I wonder about Babs's accident."

He frowned. "What do you mean?"

"I sometimes think it might have been avoided. I was behind Johnny when it happened. And it almost seemed that he deliberately shoved her."

Bill's eyes widened. "Did you mention this to Tony?"

"No."

"You should have."

Distressed, she said, "I'm not sure. It's just a hunch. And Johnny has been victimized by so many rumors before I didn't want to start another one—especially one which might be unjustified."

Bill's plain face was grim. "You're being broad-minded about him again. Just as you were when he scalded your hand!"

"That was an accident!" she protested.

"You think so?" Bill's tone was laconic.

"Because Johnny has so much going for him—wealth, stardom, and appearance—people deliberately want to hurt him in some way. That's why they've started all those rumors about him. I don't want to be unfair to him in any way."

Bill said, "Of course you don't." His tone was sarcastic. "If you have to make a choice you'd rather be unfair to poor old Babs Darriot!"

"Don't say that!" she protested.

"I think it's true," Bill told her soberly. "If you had even a hint of suspicion about that accident, you should have discussed it with Tony. We all know Johnny was jealous of Babs because her notices rivaled his. It's quite possible he *did* shove her down the stairs."

"I can't be sure that he did. His story may have been true. Perhaps he couldn't halt himself when she stopped so suddenly. I want to believe that."

"But you're not certain," Bill said with perception. "You never will be, will you? Not a happy position for you."

She gave him a resigned glance. "Let it go at that. I'd rather worry about it than accuse Johnny unjustly."

"Big of you," her companion said wryly. "I wish I was sure that Johnny could be as generous."

"Let's not talk any more about it," she begged him in a troubled voice.

"All right," Bill said. "Just one thing: I hope that I never work in a company with that fellow again. I don't like him and I don't trust him!"

She was surprised at how emphatic Bill was in his comment on Johnny Craig. She said, "I think you're overreacting in your own way. If I'm being *too* fair to him, you're being too *unfair*. People tend to go to extremes where he is concerned."

"Just the same, I'll be glad when the run is over," Bill said. "By the way I'm going to Cape Cod for the summer. I'll be stage-managing at the Dennis Playhouse."

"Wonderful," she said with sincerity.

"How about you?"

"I haven't anything lined up," she said. "Not likely there will be anything now. I've been waiting for word from my agent."

"Maybe there'll be an opening at Dennis," Bill suggested. "If there is I'll let you know."

"Thanks," she said with a smile. "I'd enjoy that."

But nothing in the way of work turned up. She talked to her New York agent on the phone. The prospects were bleak. It was during the last week of the run of the play in Boston that Johnny Craig invited her out for a drive and to have an early dinner at a favorite restaurant in Framingham.

"We'll have plenty of time to drive back and do the show," he promised her.

Because she didn't want any bad feelings between them, she agreed. He arrived at her apartment in mid-afternoon and they took a drive which finally brought them to the Maridor Restaurant in Framingham for an early dinner. It was over the table there that Johnny had a frank talk with her.

He began. "I think you've tried to avoid me most of the time we've been working together."

"You're imagining that," she told him.

"I think not," he said, his eyes fixed on her. "You've been paying too much attention to those stories they've circulated about me. In any case, it doesn't matter now. I want you to know that I like you."

"Thank you," she said quietly.

He kept studying her intently. "I'm not saying that I'm in love with you; I'm not sure of that. But I do think a lot of you and I respect your talents as an actress."

"I appreciate that," she said, amazed at why he should embark on this elaborate discussion of their relationship and his opinion of her.

He offered her a wry smile. "You don't think me an utter villain, do you?"

It was a strange question offered to her by a very complex individual. She smiled at him across the table and told him, "Of course I don't think you a villain. And I have admiration for you as an actor."

"Good," Johnny said in a businesslike tone. "You may be interested to know I had my lawyer send a good-sized check to Babs Darriot. I had a nice letter from her in return."

Kim couldn't help being impressed. "That was good of you," she said.

He shrugged. "I felt guilty about that accident. Just as I was upset about spilling that coffee over you. I seem to have a knack for causing accidents."

"I'm glad you were kind to Babs," she said. "She needed the work she lost. The money will be a big help to her."

"I covered her salary," Johnny said. "Now, about you. What are you going to do after Saturday night?"

"I have nothing lined up," she said. "Why?"

The handsome actor's eyes met hers solemnly. "Because I have an offer for you. I want you to play a part for me off-stage."

CHAPTER THREE

Kim stared at the handsome, young actor in surprise. "What are you talking about?"

He seemed amused. "I'm offering you a job of acting—only it won't be onstage."

"I know no more than before."

"I'll explain."

"I hope so." She knew he was eccentric, but this was a bit more than she'd bargained for.

Johnny Craig began to offer his explanation slowly, saying, "I'm going to spend most of the summer at the family estate on Pirate Island. The house is located just on the outskirts of the town of Dark Harbor. It's one of the few places where I know the natives and like them—a spot where I can really relax. But there is a catch."

"Oh?" She had no idea what he might be leading to.

"The catch is the girl next door," he said with a wry smile. "Her name is Sheila Moore. She's the daughter of a wealthy widower and an only child at that. For a while I thought I was in love with her. Now I'm not nearly so sure. And I think she has the same doubts about me. I don't want to spend the summer having an uneasy romance with her."

"So?"

"So I'd like to take you down there with me as my fiancée. It isn't necessary that we claim to be formally engaged, just enough to say that we hope to be married. I think this would give me a nice protection against rushing into a romance with Sheila, and it also would give her a chance to show whether she really cares for me or not. I'll pay you to act the role of my girlfriend—without any obligations. When I leave Dark Harbor the engagement would end."

She stared at him. "It's an amazing offer."

"It's a solid one."

"This Sheila Moore must be repulsive or you wouldn't be looking for protection from her," Kim said.

"On the contrary," he said, "she's a beautiful brunette with a gorgeous figure and she's smart. She has a law degree."

Kim was further surprised. "And yet you aren't sure that you are in love with her?"

"Let's say I want to be very sure before I commit myself. Our families have encouraged the match, and that may have put me off it."

"I see," she said. "So you propose to hire me as a buffer. And you hope to prove through my being there that your romance with this Sheila is truly an important one?"

He nodded. "That's about it."

"There's a catch," she said, looking at him directly. "Suppose I should fall desperately in love with you while I'm acting the role. What then?"

"I wouldn't mind," Johnny Craig said. "It could be that *we* are the ones who should fall in love. If I find that I'm turning to you rather than Sheila, I'll let you know."

She raised a staying hand. "I haven't said I'd take on the job yet."

"You will," he said with a smile.

Her eyebrows lifted. "How can you be so positive?"

"The challenge interests you."

"Don't be so sure of that," she said. "It would mean living in the same house with your family, keeping up the pretense for them. I'm not sure I'm equal to it. I'd be too uncomfortable."

"Not if you gave yourself to the role," he argued. "You

can name your own salary."

Kim felt the offer absurd. It seemed to her the best way to handle it was to name a truly fantastic salary. So she did, saying, "That is my best price."

To her utter shock Johnny Craig didn't blink an eyelid. He said, "Agreed. I'll pay you that figure. You'll get the money a week in advance directly from me in a plain envelope. No one but you and I will know of the arrangement."

Confused, she exclaimed, "You haven't given me any time to think it over!"

"It's all settled," he said with another of his wry smiles.

"What will I tell other people?" she wanted to know. "I must be able to offer some reason for going to your place for the summer."

"Easy," said Johnny, who seemed to have worked out an answer to all her objections in advance. "You will say that you are going to Dark Harbor to act as companion to my mother. She has had several in the past, but at the moment the post is vacant. It all fits in."

Kim gave him a resigned look. "You have everything worked out! I can't believe it!"

"It's important to me," Johnny said. "I had to work out every detail to be sure you'd accept."

So it was settled. When Bill Griffith learned that she was going to the Craig mansion at Dark Harbor to be companion to Johnny's mother, he expressed surprise.

"I can't imagine you taking such a job," he protested.

"It will give me a summer's work," she said. "I have no theater job lined up."

"You could go back to New York and Gimbel's," he said.

"Not in this hot weather," she told him. "And we won't be all that far apart. You may be able to come over and see me weekends."

"I still don't like the idea," Bill grumbled. "Especially knowing that Johnny will be around you all the time."

"I can handle Johnny Craig," she said confidently, although truthfully she wasn't by any means that sure.

The Sunday after the play closed in Boston Johnny came for her in a Mercedes convertible and they began the drive down to Cape Cod. They didn't talk much along the way. Kim was extremely tense. At Hyannis they waited for the ferry and boarded the early evening run. With the car stowed safely below, they found a place at the railing of the main deck and watched Cape Cod fade into the distance as they sailed out toward Pirate Island.

Johnny smiled at her as they leaned against the railing. "You will have to show a little more animation when we reach my place. I'll want you to be more excited as a young woman in love should be."

"I'll manage," she promised him. "Just now we can be ourselves and relax."

"Of course," he said. "And when you meet Sheila, be nice to her, but let her get the impression you're willing to put up a fight for me."

She said, "My task becomes more complicated all the time."

"Not really," the young man protested. "The things I've told you constitute the main points."

"I still may change my mind about this," she warned him.

"You mustn't," he said. "I need you."

It was nearly two hours later that the island came in sight. Johnny pointed out the town called Dark Harbor to her. He said, "Our house is on a cliff facing the ocean. You'll be able to spot it as we enter the harbor."

Kim's uneasiness grew as they neared the island. She had taken on a secret task which she was not sure she could carry out. Johnny's idea of using her to test and perhaps taunt this other girl was a weird one such as you might expect from him. Only a person of his immense ego would hit on such a plan.

Worst of all she was apprehensive of how the family would greet her. She had taken them for a close, clannish unit and she feared they might bitterly resent her, especially if they had encouraged this romance between Johnny and the other girl. Her position in the old mansion could be most uncomfortable.

She asked Johnny, "Will my arrival be a surprise to your family?"

"No," he said with one of his smug smiles. "I've talked to Mother on the phone. She'll even have a room prepared for you."

"How did she react on the phone?"

Johnny laughed. "She said she wasn't all that much surprised. She had an idea we were heading for a romance."

"She met me only that once! How could she think that?"

"I don't know," he said. "Anyway I'm satisfied that she is prepared to accept our story. She told me that Sheila was home waiting for me to arrive and said she'd be sure to be disappointed."

Kim looked at him in awe. "You are cruel!" she accused him. "I shouldn't help you torture that poor girl."

"Sheila can look after herself," he said. "This way we'll be sure to find out who really cares for whom."

"I'm completely confused," Kim admitted.

As they entered the harbor Johnny pointed out different areas of the island. "The mountain is called Bald Mountain," he told her. "The rest of the land is level, although cliffs border on the ocean."

"How did the island get its name?" she asked.

"In the old days pirates used it as a place to rendezvous.

Rumors of buried treasure here have never been borne out although many have searched for it," the actor said. "After the pirates came the Puritan farmers, and the whaling ships. My ancestors made their fortune in whaling and built the family mansion here."

"Those must have been exciting days."

Johnny's handsome face lit up. "A century or so ago this harbor was a forest of masts of whalers. There are records to show that as many as a hundred ships were packed along the wharves at one time. And the wharves were covered with endless rows of barrels containing sperm oil. Even before the Revolutionary War, this island furnished oil for half the capitals of the civilized world. Candles made here were sold from Lisbon to Singapore and fine ladies used Pirate Island whalebone for their corsets and had their handkerchiefs scented with perfume made from Dark Harbor ambergris."

She listened to him in amazement. "You really get excited about it, don't you?"

He nodded. "I do. You wouldn't guess the history this place has from the few fishing boats and pleasure craft gathered here now."

Kim studied the numerous small craft on the blue waters. "There seem to be a lot of boats here to me. But then I'm no judge."

"Nothing compared to the old days," he assured her.

The ferry slowed down now, its motors pounding more slowly as they drew near the Dark Harbor wharf.

Standing with Johnny in the bow of the ship she had her first glimpse of Dark Harbor. There seemed to be a wide street rising from the wharf. The houses on either side of the street and along the wharf front were gray and weatherbeaten. They huddled together as if on guard against the onslaught of ocean storms. There were a group of people on the wharf waiting for the ferry's arrival and a number of cars parked in the background.

Johnny gave her one of his crooked smiles. "Well, we've arrived. I hope you're going to like Dark Harbor."

"I'm terribly nervous about all this," she told him.

"Don't think about it," he told her. "Live your part as you do onstage."

"I'm onstage only for a limited time," she reminded him. "This masquerade is to go on for the summer."

"You'll enjoy it," he promised.

By no means sure that she would, she accompanied him off the ferry to the wharf where they waited for the Mercedes to be driven off. The pungent odor of the salt air filled her nostrils and made her feel very much alive. It was a pleasant evening and the island had a picturesque air about it.

She told the actor, "It is a lovely, peaceful spot."

"At one time there were no automobiles allowed here," he said. "And there wasn't any electricity. Now we have lots of cars and paved roads and a central electric plant along with a public water system."

"Progress," she said. "I suppose it has its good points along with its bad."

Johnny was watching the cars come off. He said, "Personally, I'd like it to be as backward and isolated as possible. That's the best hope of retaining the charm of the island."

A spare, white-haired man with a slight stoop and wearing a captain's cap had been standing watching them and now he came over with a smile on his pleasant, weathered face.

"Good evening, Johnny," he said in an ancient voice. His blue eyes under shaggy white brows had a twinkle in them. "Didn't know you were due back for the summer."

"Captain Zack!" Johnny said in a delighted voice and he went to the old man and shook hands vigorously with him.

Then he turned to her and said, "Kim Rice, I want you to meet Captain Zachary Miller, one of the island's oldest citizens and a good friend of mine!"

"I'm glad to meet you, Captain Miller," she said.

"Likewise," the captain said. "This your first visit to the island?"

"Yes," she replied. "I'm looking forward to seeing it all."

Johnny gave her a teasing glance and then told the old man, "Kim and I plan to be married a little later on."

Zachary Miller showed mild surprise. "Well, what do you know? Figured that you'd get around to that one day. You still in show business?"

"Yes," Johnny said. "And Kim is also an actress."

"That fits," the old man said. "My missus came from a family of seafaring men so she understood my work. Best to marry someone who understands what you're doing."

Johnny laughed. "I agree. What are you doing this summer, captain?"

"I'm officially retired," the old man said. "But Derek Mills at the museum came to see me and he's arranged for me to give a couple of lectures a week up there for the tourists. I'm giving them a talk on the old whaling days and I mention your great-grandfather's part in the trade."

"I must come up and hear you," Johnny said.

The old man chuckled. "Do that," he said. "And I'll introduce you to my audience. They'll enjoy meeting a famous movie star."

Johnny turned to Kim and said, "The museum is one of the main places of interest. They have a wonderful collection of sailing ships and marine life."

"I'll want to see it," she said.

"Go up any time," the sprightly old captain said. "Derek Mills is a fine fellow and he'll show you around himself if you tell him you're a friend of mine."

"I'll do that," she said.

Johnny said, "What about Derek Mills? Has he married again?"

"Not yet," the old man replied. "Though he sure enough could if he wanted to. Plenty of gals have set their caps for him. He's handsome enough and has plenty of money."

"I know," Johnny said. "I think the tragedy of his wife's illness and death hit him harder than most people guessed."

"I agree," Captain Miller said. He nodded pleasantly to Kim. "I'll look forward to seeing you again, Miss Rice." And he left them to walk up the wharf toward the parked cars.

Kim said, "He's a nice old man. So bright."

"And a lot older than you'd guess," Johnny told her. Then he pointed to the area of the wharf where the cars were being delivered. "Our wait is over. There's our car now."

They drove up the cobblestoned Main Street. Kim forgot her nervousness in her enjoyment of the quaint old town. Johnny was at his best as he pointed out an ancient inn known as the Green Heron which he said had been operated by a Kimble family down through the years. There was a tavern in connection with the inn and it had a battered sign with a faded green heron on it. Kim found the town like a movie set for a New England film.

They drove along a side street and onto a road which seemed to follow the shoreline. Johnny told her, "This road runs all the way to the end of the island, where an old monastery is located. It used to be a leper hospital."

"A leper hospital!" she exclaimed in astonishment.

"Yes," he said, busy at the wheel. "A ship was wrecked off the island more than a century ago and many of its crew remained here to become part of the colony. But a number of them turned out to be afflicted with leprosy and passed the disease on to a good percentage of the villagers. It was a bad business until the monks volunteered to look after the sufferers and set up a hospital in the monastery for them. It later became a government hospital for lepers."

"Are there any lepers there now?"

"No. Leprosy has been largely conquered. The monks long ago sold the monastery. It was taken over by a weird hippie group for a year or so, and then a millionaire bought it. He has converted it into a swank summer home. It's still an interesting place to visit."

Kim said, "The island has had an interesting history."

"It's one of the things I like about it," he said. They turned off the main roadway and drove through stone gateposts along a much narrower gravel road. This eventually brought them to the front door of the Craig mansion which rose majestically on a cliff above the ocean. The pounding of the surf could be clearly heard as Johnny helped Kim out of the car.

She gave him a frightened look. "I'm going to need some support now," she warned him.

"Let's find out how good an actress you really are," he said. "The servants will bring our bags in." And he led her to the front steps.

The ordeal was minor compared to what she'd feared. Johnny's mother and father received her coolly, but in a friendly enough manner. She suspected that they were not capable of any real warmth. Within a short time she was installed in a large bedroom with its own attached bathroom which looked out on the ocean. She guessed this was the choice of the guest bedrooms and so felt honored.

Johnny seemed amused by the entire charade. He stayed in her room long enough to see that everything was satisfactory and then went on to his own room, telling her that he would see her downstairs when she'd unpacked.

She went about the task of settling in as quickly as she could. They had eaten on the ferry, so she wasn't hungry. After she freshened up, she made her way downstairs to find Johnny and Irma in serious conversation in the living room.

As soon as Irma noticed her enter the room, she broke off her conversation with Johnny and came over to greet her. With a smile, Irma said, "So Johnny coaxed you into coming here. I'm thrilled about the news. And I'm certain you'll both be very happy."

"Thanks," Kim said uneasily, not helped by Johnny standing in the background smiling smugly.

"You may find it quiet here," Irma warned her. "There isn't too much social life. But the air and the ocean are wonderful. I always leave here feeling as if my health had been restored."

"I'm already fascinated with what I've seen of the island," Kim said.

"There's plenty more to show you," Johnny promised.

Irma gave him a look of sisterly affection. "It is so good to have Johnny back here. He stayed only a week or so last summer, and I was afraid this year he wouldn't come at all."

Johnny's eyes held a roguish twinkle. "That was before I met Kim and fell in love."

"And about time," Irma said. Then she looked a trifle uneasy as she added, "By the way, Sheila heard that you were arriving tonight and she invited us all over there."

He suddenly showed dismay. "No!"

"I'm afraid so," Irma said. "I didn't know what to do. So I said I thought you could come." She turned to Kim. "It's a little awkward. I imagine Johnny has explained to you about Sheila."

"Just a little," she said, blushing.

Irma sighed. "Sheila has always carried a torch for Johnny.

It began when we were children playing here during our summer vacations. I expected she would grow out of it since Johnny obviously never cared for her in the same way. But she hasn't. And I honestly think she still has hopes—even though I've told her about you."

Johnny looked a little relieved. "At least I'm glad she has heard about Kim."

"I told her as soon as you phoned," his attractive sister said. "I thought it only right. She has clung to her illusions too long."

"Right," Johnny said.

"I'm going upstairs for a moment," Irma went on. "Jim Blake will be coming to join me and go over to Sheila's. I understand she's having a few other people to welcome you."

"I might have guessed," Johnny said with a small groan.

Irma laughed. "Well, now you know the worst!" And with that she left them to go upstairs.

As soon as she had gone Kim turned to Johnny in mild despair. "Johnny, I don't feel up to going over there."

He said, "It's part of the performance."

"I don't care," she protested.

"There's nothing to worry about," he assured her. "Sheila will be a fine hostess. She may gently show you her claws, but it will all be very polite. You can be sure she has asked us over just for the purpose of seeing you and sizing you up."

"I don't want to be sized up!" she exclaimed with distaste.

He raised a reminding finger. "Part of the job."

She shook her head. "I shouldn't have come here!"

"Nonsense," he told her. "This will be the easiest and most pleasant summer's work you've ever had."

"Not if what has happened this evening is a sample," she said bitterly.

Johnny chuckled and came and put his arm around her.

"Just remember you're doing everyone a good turn by being here. It may be that I'll decide I do care enough for Sheila to marry her. And if you make her sufficiently jealous, she may be willing to put up with me as a difficult husband. You're spreading sweetness and light all around."

"I don't see it that way," she argued. "I can't imagine what your family thinks of me."

"They think you're about ready to take their troublesome son off their hands, and that alone is enough to earn their gratitude," he joked.

Jim Blake arrived and said the proper, pleasant things to her by way of greeting. A few minutes later Irma came downstairs again in a different yellow dress and all four of them crossed the lawn and took a shortcut through a barrier of tall evergreens which brought them out on the lawn of the adjoining mansion. It was also of gray stone, but of a less imposing design than the Craig home.

Rather than entering the house, they went around to steps leading to a large, screened veranda. A party was going on in this ample space and a tense Kim saw that Madeline and Stephen Craig were already there. Johnny's parents had glasses in their hands and were talking to a handsome, serious-looking man with light brown hair.

A slim, pretty girl with jet black hair and liquid green eyes came to greet them as they entered the veranda. She was wearing a black dress with a quantity of fringe on it that cried out of being the work of a prominent designer. She had been smoking, and now she held her cigarette rather awkwardly as she thrust her lips up for Johnny to kiss.

"Johnny, darling," she said in a languid voice. "How good to have you back."

"Sheila!" he said and bent to kiss the black-haired girl briefly. Then he turned to Kim and said, "This is Kim!"

Sheila's eyes widened with seeming delight. "You're so cute!" she said in her lazy fashion. "I had no idea you'd be so cute. And I hear you are an actress?"

"Yes," Kim said, almost fiercely, her one desire to turn and race out of the veranda.

"Well, you must tell me all about it," Sheila said. She gave Johnny a reproving glance. "Johnny is so reluctant to share any of his theater experiences with me."

Johnny grimaced. "You're not interested in theater and you know it!"

"You're so wrong!" Sheila said with an attractive pout. "I like to go to the theater. I saw *Hair* and *Oh, Calcutta* and just a few weeks ago I saw that new musical in the Village, *Let My People Come!* So don't say I'm not a theater buff."

Johnny laughed. "I won't, since all the shows you went to see were played in the buff. You're not a fan for theater: your thing is nudity!"

"You're wicked!" Sheila said with a tiny laugh. "Now I want Kim to meet some of my guests. You already know Johnny's parents, but you haven't met these others."

"Don't worry about me," Kim protested. "I can't stay long. Johnny can get me a drink."

Sheila had her by the arm. "But you must mingle and meet these people. They are friends of Johnny's. I hope you don't mind that we have only candles out here on the porch. I like it when it is almost dark like this, don't you?"

"It's pleasant," Kim agreed. It was true that the near darkness of the porch left her feeling somewhat less nervous.

Sheila took her up to a distinguished, gray-haired man with horn-rimmed glasses. She said, "This is Dr. Henry Taylor, the best doctor we have on the island. I want you to meet Kim Rice, doctor."

The doctor shook hands with Kim and jovially informed

her, "The reason I'm the best doctor on the island is that most of the time I'm the only one."

Sheila said, "He's being properly modest. He's done wonderful things for us summer people, and he stays here all winter to care for the fisher folk. That's dedication!"

Johnny arrived at this moment and thrust a drink in Kim's hand. At the same time he said, "Hello, doctor."

"Hello, Johnny," the elderly doctor said. "Good to have you back again."

Sheila went on. "Dr. Taylor has built a small hospital for his patients here."

"That is wonderful," Kim said.

The doctor sighed. "There are a lot of improvements I'd like to make, still."

"When I think of the old days," Sheila said, shaking her head. "Dr. Taylor looked after us when we were mere babies. There's not much he doesn't know about us. And he played a part in a major tragedy we experienced when we were teenagers."

Johnny's face was not plainly visible in the shadows of the porch but his voice was taut as he said, "No one wants to hear about that again!"

"But Kim has never heard about it," Sheila protested. "I think she ought to know something about the past since she's going to be one of us." She turned to Kim and went on. "There was a girl from Rhode Island used to come here every summer. Pretty child, as I remember. She played with us and she used to like to tease Johnny."

Johnny said, "Excuse me!" in a taut voice and he moved away.

Sheila glanced after him and in a lower voice, said, "Johnny is sensitive about this. He hated to be teased, but I think he was fond of that girl. One day when they were out alone together, walking along the edge of a gravel pit, she lost her footing and fell over the side. An avalanche of the gravel covered her in seconds. Johnny came running screaming to the house! My father phoned for Dr. Taylor, but by the time he got to the pit and the girl's body was uncovered, the doctor could do nothing."

Dr. Taylor nodded. "I remember it well. I was too late that time."

Sheila said, "All a part of our past. A lot of odd things have happened on this island, Kim."

Kim swallowed hard. "Yes," she said stiffly. "I can well imagine it." And she felt a cold chill down her spine. She was convinced that Sheila had deliberately brought up this story to torment Johnny, who had walked away from the telling of it.

Even more frightening, she had the idea Sheila meant the story to have a dimension which the friendly Dr. Taylor seemed not to have noticed. Sheila had stressed that the girl who was killed had teased Johnny, and she had also stressed that they were alone when the accident happened. It almost appeared that she'd been covertly hinting that Johnny in one of his rages had shoved the girl down into the gravel pit and so caused her death.

As these thoughts coursed through Kim's mind, Sheila said, "There is someone else you must meet, but before I introduce you, let me give you a word of advice."

She glanced at the girl nervously. "Advice?"

"Yes," Sheila said solemnly. "Don't cross Johnny in anything!"

"Why do you say that?" It seemed that this was a confirmation of the ugly story the black-haired girl had told earlier—a confirmation that Johnny had at least indirectly once killed someone.

"When I was just a child—ten or so, maybe nine—I played a trick on Johnny. He found out about it."

"Oh?"

Sheila nodded. And in a solemn voice she added, "I had a pet cat. A few days later, someone hanged it. I found it hanging in an outbuilding. I ran off to the woods and threw up!"

Kim was shocked. "Are you saying that Johnny did it?"

"I don't know," Sheila said. "I only know that young boys can be terribly cruel. And I've taken no chances in all the years since. I've been careful not to have any real battle with Johnny."

Kim listened to the attractive girl's words in numbed terror. She could only hope that it was a vicious trick on the part of this girl who was still in love with Johnny. A cruel deception meant on this first night of her being on the island to make her afraid of the man to whom she was supposed to be engaged. Otherwise the remarks were far too obvious.

Summoning all her resources of poise, she said, "Your stories are macabre, but I can't see that they have any bearing on Johnny. I'm surprised that you associate him with such happenings. You must have had so many pleasant times together."

"We *have* had," Sheila at once said contritely. "I'm sorry I said those things. I guess I got carried away. And we do tend to recall unpleasant things more easily than the pleasant ones."

"I know," Kim said.

"Here is Derek Mills," Sheila said as they came up to the serious, brown-haired man who had earlier been talking to Johnny's parents. She introduced Kim to the youngish director of the island's museum.

Kim told him, "I've already heard about you from Captain Zachary Miller."

Derek laughed pleasantly. "You've been on the island only a short time and you've already met the captain! Well, that figures. He is probably the most interesting man on the island, and he likes pretty girls."

She said, "I understand he is lecturing for you."

"That was an accomplishment," Derek Mills said with some pride. "He is a marvelous raconteur, and he never would do it before."

"I must go hear him."

"Do," the museum director urged. "Come by the museum anytime and I'll be glad to show you around."

"Thank you," she said.

"Have you known Johnny Craig long?" Derek Mills asked.

There was a kind of concerned interest in his question which puzzled her. He made it seem almost like a warning. She could not see his face clearly in the shadowed atmosphere of the porch, so she could not be certain of this. The few candles were set out by the makeshift bar and so did not spread their glow around.

She said, "I met him a few weeks ago when we played together in a theater in Boston."

"A sudden romance," Derek Mills said.

"You might call it that."

The serious young man said, "I'm glad Johnny has finally made his mind up about someone. I've been rather worried about him. We grew up together, and he has always been a kind of loner. I was older than he, of course."

"Not much," Kim said.

"Not much," Derek Mills agreed. "But at the growing-up age, it made enough difference that we weren't close friends."

Johnny came up by them, seeming to have recovered from his annoyance. In an easy tone, he said, "What are you two talking about?"

She turned to him. "Nothing important."

Sheila came out of the darkness to stand with them. She took a position between Johnny and Kim. In her lazy drawl she asked Kim, "How do you like the magnificent Craig mansion by the sea?"

"Very much, what I've seen of it," she said. "It's really a kind of castle."

"You may well say that," Sheila agreed. "And you know it has everything that a castle should have—including a ghost!"

CHAPTER FOUR

From Johnny Craig's lips there came an almost agonized "Sheila—must you?"

Even though they were all standing there in near darkness, Kim was well aware of the young actor's upset emotional state. She was sure this was another of Sheila's deliberate acts to make her ill at ease and torture Johnny.

Sheila's tone was mocking as she said, "My ghost story isn't all *that* bad."

Derek Mills now spoke up, saying, "I had no idea there was a ghost associated with Craig House, though I must say I'm not surprised, nearly every old house on the island has some legend of a phantom attached to it."

Sheila turned to the pleasant museum director. "This isn't one of your ancient ghosts, Derek; this one is of recent vintage."

"Really?" Derek Mills sounded interested.

Sheila gave her attention to Kim again, saying, "The ghost shows itself here on certain moonlit nights, both at Craig House and our grounds—a phantom figure of a young woman in a tight dress of shimmering black sequins drenched with the ocean waters and with wisps of seaweed caught in her hair and plastered to her lovely face."

"No one is interested in your story!" Johnny said painfully.

"I'm sure you're wrong," Sheila went on in the same mocking tone. "Wouldn't you like to know who the ghost is, Kim?"

Kim said, "I suppose so. Do you know?"

"I knew her very well in life," Sheila said. "She was a girl employed in the island's only smart boutique. She enjoyed parties and drinking, perhaps too much. Because she was a beauty, she was invited everywhere. Her name was Helen Walsh. You remember her, Johnny!"

"I've heard enough of your ghost story," Johnny said in a grim voice and moved away.

Sheila gave a mirthless little laugh. "Well, I didn't think he was so touchy. He did know Helen well enough; he often dated her."

Derek Mills spoke again. "This is the same Helen Walsh who was drowned while out on the big pleasure boat *Victoria* a couple of years ago?"

"Right," Sheila said with satisfaction. "A group of us—including Helen—had hired the *Victoria* for a moonlight excursion. There was drinking and dancing. When the boat docked, Helen was missing. Her body was never found. The assumption was that she'd had too much to drink, become sick, and fallen over the side."

"I remember the whole business," Derek Mills said in a troubled voice. "There was a lot of gossip at the time. Until you mentioned the girl's name, it didn't come back to me. So Helen Walsh is your ghost?"

"Yes. I've seen her at least a half-dozen times," Sheila said. "I understand the boat was almost opposite this part of the coastline when she went overboard, so it is only natural that her phantom figure should emerge from the water here."

"Has anyone else seen this ghost?" Derek Mills asked.

"No," Sheila admitted. "But others will see it as time goes on."

"That's a remarkable story," Kim acknowledged.

"Yes. I can't think why Johnny's so thin-skinned about it."

"He was a friend of the drowned girl," Derek Mills pointed out.

"So was I," Sheila said promptly. "I can't see any harm in my mentioning it. Can you, Kim?"

With the question so bluntly put to her, Kim searched for some sort of reasonable reply. She said, "Different people react to things in different ways. I suspect Johnny must have liked the girl a great deal."

"I had an idea she was only a passing fancy with him," was Sheila's reply.

"I suppose we'll never really know the truth since she's dead," Kim replied quietly.

"Your story interests me," Derek Mills told Sheila. "If you want to write down the circumstances of your seeing the phantom and send the paper to me at the museum, I'll file it."

Sheila's manner was derisive. "All you museum people think of are your records."

"If someone didn't think of them, there wouldn't be any history of the island," Derek pointed out.

"I suppose not," the girl said impatiently. "But really, your reply was so typical I couldn't let it pass by."

"May as well add your ghost story to the others," Derek said and then, turning to Kim, he added, "You won't forget to come see me at the museum, will you?"

"I won't," she promised. She had liked the pleasant stranger even under the difficult conditions of their meeting. Everyone was so tense it was impossible to relax and enjoy the conversation.

"I must be going now," Derek Mills told Sheila. She at once expressed regrets and escorted him to the veranda steps.

Kim found herself standing alone for a moment. Then she saw a figure approaching her in the dark shadows. It was the lawyer, Jim Blake, to whom Johnny's sister Irma was apparently engaged.

The lawyer halted at her side and asked, "Did Sheila give you a bad time?"

She said, "Why do you ask that?"

"I expected she would," Jim Blake said frankly. "You're not the summer visitor she was hoping to have, you know. She seems to have made up her mind she's going to marry Johnny. Your arrival on the scene had to be a blow."

Kim said, "She seemed to bother Johnny more than she did me."

"So that's how she worked it. What did she say?"

Rather annoyed at his inquisitive line of conversation, Kim was tempted to turn away and not answer. But she decided this would only cause more unpleasantness at a time when she could ill afford it. So she said, "Sheila upset him by telling a ghost story."

Jim Blake seemed shocked. "Did she go into that business about seeing Helen Walsh step out of the ocean?"

"Yes."

"Mighty bad taste," the lawyer said. "She could have saved that for some other time."

"Then you've heard the story?"

"More than once," Jim said in a wry voice. "She's been setting everyone's nerves on edge with it. And, oddly enough, she is the only one who has seen the ghost."

"Oh?"

"We all knew Helen Walsh," the lawyer went on. "I won't say she was a particular friend, but she was included in a lot of the parties—one of the town girls who was accepted by the summer social set. Johnny used to chat with her whenever she was at a party. And I think it was because Sheila was jealous of her and Johnny that she started this ghost-story thing. The whole point is to taunt Johnny."

"Why should it bother him so much?" Kim asked.

Jim Blake shrugged. "I think he feels it is unfair of Sheila to go on as she does. He probably liked Helen, considers her drowning a tragic accident, and feels it should be let go at that. Sheila, by continually bringing up this ghost thing, is keeping the whole affair very much alive."

"So there you are!" It was the voice of Irma as she joined them.

Jim turned to her and said, "I was just explaining to Kim about the Helen Walsh thing."

"The ghost story!" Irma said in a bored voice. "Sheila must be at her worst tonight to saddle you with that sad yarn." And to Jim, she added, "I think we should go. My parents have already left."

"Good idea," Jim said. He glanced across the veranda at the bar with its lighted candles and said to Kim, "Johnny is over there, drinking too much. Why don't you rescue him and bring him back to the house for dinner?"

"All right," she said, and left them to hurry across to Johnny who stood apart, with a glass tilted to his lips. She touched his arm and told him, "Time to leave."

Johnny slowly put down the glass and turned to her. It was at once obvious that he'd been drinking far too much. His eyes were glassy and he stared at her for a moment before he answered her.

"Time to leave?" he echoed her.

"Yes."

"Okay," he said. His face was grim. "I hope you enjoyed yourself."

"I might have if you had remained with me and not had so much to drink," she told him.

He looked grim and gazed across the shadows where

Sheila was saying good night to departing guests. He said, "Sorry. But I didn't much care for the conversation."

"So I gathered."

Johnny gave her a drunken glance. "You don't know anything about it!"

"I think I know enough," she said. "Now let's go. Please don't make a scene!"

"Make a scene!" Johnny laughed incredulously. "That's good! After the way Sheila has behaved tonight! You tell me not to make a scene!" And he laughed again drunkenly.

Kim linked her arm in his and led him across to the exit. Sheila was standing there ready to bid them good-bye. She said, "Can't you two stay and join Father and me for a bite to eat? I'd hoped that you'd stay for dinner so I could get to know you better, Kim."

Kim shook her head. "Not tonight, thanks. Another time. We enjoyed your party."

Sheila smiled gaily. "How nice of you to say so! I want to see you again—soon!"

Johnny stood there, swaying a little with a surly look fixed on his handsome face. "Thanks," he said in a bitter voice. "Thanks for everything."

"It's so nice having you back, Johnny!" Sheila exclaimed, ignoring his condition and the tone of his thank-you, as she quickly reached up and gave him a peck on the cheek.

Kim was afraid for a moment that Johnny would strike Sheila. She hastily moved him on, down the veranda steps which he negotiated with some difficulty. Then they were moving across the lawn and towards the shortcut through the evergreens to Craig House. Only then did Kim feel some relief.

As they walked, she said, "You don't get along well with Sheila."

"You think not?" Johnny said.

"I'm amazed. I understood you two were very close. You don't give that impression. You act as if you hate each other."

Johnny stumbled along the path. "Tonight was different."

"It must have been," she said ruefully. "I never want to go through such an experience again."

"I'm paying you well enough."

"Not for evenings like that," she said. "Just a little more, and you'll have my notice."

"Everybody likes you," Johnny said. "You showed Sheila up with your quiet dignity."

"I was struck dumb by her accounts of your cruelty and your drowned girlfriends!"

Johnny turned to her. "Don't you start!"

"Sorry," she said. "I didn't realize that was such a no-no."

"You don't know anything about it," Johnny said, his voice slurred.

Ahead, the great old mansion rose like a gray wraith against the dark, star-studded sky. Lights blazed at many of the windows of the stone house, giving it a warmly welcoming air. Johnny paused when he was about thirty feet from the front entrance and stood, swaying a little. He seemed attempting to sober up, but he had drunk far too much.

She gazed up at him with anxious eyes. "Do you feel well?"

"Give me a minute," he said dully.

"This is awful. To have you like this on our first night here!"

"They've seen me like this before!"

"I don't care," she said. "You're making it a lot harder for me. I should never have agreed to come here. I knew what you were like from Boston."

A sudden rage seemed to take hold of him and he reached

out and seized her arm in a viselike grip as he harshly demanded, "What am I like?"

She tried to draw away, but couldn't. Hot pain seared through her arm. Her eyes were frightened as she stared at him and said, "You're not dependable! I can't guess what you'll do next!"

He eyed her drunkenly and then loosened his grip on her arm so that she was able to free herself. "I don't mind if that's the worst you say about me!"

She warned him. "When you are sober in the morning, we'll talk. I think I'll leave tomorrow."

Johnny was now gazing past her, out across the water at a beam of light which was sweeping the ocean, moving back and forth in an arc. He said, "That's Gull's Point Light! Warns of the shoal out there."

For a moment Kim felt sorry for him. She knew that Sheila had deliberately set out to upset him and ruin her introduction to Dark Harbor. She touched the handsome young actor on the arm. "Do you feel all right to go on inside now?"

He looked at her again. "Yes. I think so."

They moved on towards the front steps and went inside. The moment he entered the big reception hall he halted again. She asked him, "Are you feeling ill?"

"Dizzy," he said. "I can't make dinner. You go on in. I'll go up to my room."

"I won't know what to say!" she protested. "What will I tell them?"

"Tell them I'm drunk," Johnny said almost harshly as he lurched away from her. He barely made the stairway and grasped the railing with a deathlike intensity and slowly mounted the stairs. Watching him, she knew it was hopeless. In a matter of minutes he would throw himself on his bed and pass out.

She was standing there debating what she would do next when Johnny's austere, white-haired mother came out of the living room to join her. Madeline Craig had an anxious look on her worn face.

She asked, "What happened to my son?"

Kim said, "He has a headache. He's decided to skip dinner."

"Did he tell you that?" Mrs. Craig seemed to doubt it.

"I'm afraid so," she said. "I'm sorry."

Johnny's mother glanced up the stairway with a troubled uncertainty about her. Then she sighed and said, "Well, I'm sure he knows best. We'll simply have to have dinner without him."

"Yes," she said quietly. And she began to worry about what she might be asked at the dinner table.

Kim managed all right because all the others were in such a state of tension. It was clear that Sheila's cocktail party had been an ordeal for all of them. They sat around the table as the servants supplied the various courses. Their conversation was diffident and of the most casual nature.

In a strange way, Kim had the feeling that she was not the only one playing a part. It struck her that all the others were acting out a drama of their own as well. It was almost as if she were taking on a role in a play with a script unknown to her. The reticence shown by Johnny's father and mother and the quiet casualness of his sister, Irma, and the lawyer, Jim Blake, did not seem quite normal.

Kim thought there was a lot of irony in this. She had come to Craig House as a paid pretender. For some obscure reason of his own, Johnny had wanted to taunt Sheila Moore. Bringing a new girlfriend on the scene had been his idea of doing it. He'd succeeded only too well. Sheila had turned on him bitterly and made it unpleasant for all the family.

At this moment, Kim felt that the best thing she could do was have a serious talk with Johnny when he was sober the following morning and take the ferry back to the mainland. Dark Harbor had been a disaster for her. She did not think he'd been wise in the attempted charade. She felt no responsibility for protecting him from Sheila. Once she was gone, Johnny and Sheila could work out their romance the best way they liked. It meant nothing to her.

Stephen Craig gave her a gracious glance. "You are extremely quiet, Miss Rice. One does not look for that in a stage person."

She smiled bleakly. "You'd be surprised at how many of us are shy."

"We're all more shattered than shy after that performance Sheila Moore gave tonight," Irma said bitterly over her dessert.

Her mother gave her a reproving look. "I'm sure Sheila was tired, or she wouldn't have been so boring. You mustn't judge her too harshly, Irma."

Irma grimaced. "She deliberately wanted to make everyone uncomfortable, going on in that ridiculous way about Helen Walsh's ghost."

"I pay no attention to such nonsense," the patrician Stephen Craig said.

"But Johnny does!" Irma said. "It always upsets him. Sheila knows that Helen and Johnny dated. He felt very badly when she was drowned and he hates hearing it talked about. The ghost thing is the last word!"

Jim Blake nodded from his place at the table. "Especially since she seems to be the only one who has ever seen this phantom from the ocean."

"There is no phantom!" Irma said, her attractive face twisted with scorn. "You should know that! She just makes these ghost stories up to annoy us!"

Madeline Craig's pale, lined face was bleak. "She surely takes a strange way to do it."

Irma said, "She's burned up because Johnny has come back engaged to Kim."

Kim broke in, "We're not engaged. We are good friends with an understanding."

Irma waved her to silence. "The same thing. So now Sheila is going to be *twice* as difficult as ever!"

Stephen Craig cleared his throat and touched his napkin to his lips. In his sonorous voice, he said, "My son was never engaged to Sheila. Why should she care who he wants to marry?"

"Because she wanted to marry him!" Irma said scornfully. "You know that, Father. Sheila has chased Johnny all through the years—and the dreadful part of it is that he has never liked her all that well."

"I don't think this a suitable subject for the dinner table or to bother Miss Rice with," Johnny's mother said primly. "Surely there must be something else for us to discuss!"

Jim Blake, looked embarrassed, and then said, "I hear the monastery will be on sale soon."

"Is that so?" Stephen Craig said. "Those people who have it are going to give it up?"

"Yes," Jim Blake said. "They have another place at Falmouth and they've decided they don't need this one."

Madeline Craig considered this and placidly said, "I must say I could never live in that huge old building. To know that it was once a hospital for lepers would make me always most uncomfortable—not to mention the hippies who took it over a few years ago. Weren't there actually murders there?"

"Yes, Mother," Irma said resignedly, "there were murders there."

"Well, it wouldn't be a place I'd want to live," Madeline Craig repeated.

Stephen Craig glanced down the table at Kim and asked her, "Have you heard the history of the monastery?"

"Briefly," she said. "I mean to go have a look at it."

"You must," Johnny's father said. "Not a lovely building, but imposing."

At last the dinner ended. The elder Craigs politely excused themselves and went upstairs. As Kim moved into the living room, she heard the grandfather clock in the reception hall strike nine-thirty. She suddenly realized that it had been a trying day and evening. She was feeling tired.

Jim Blake and Irma followed her into the living room. The volatile Irma spread her hands in a gesture of resignation as she told Kim, "Whenever Johnny gets drunk, Father and Mother act like they did tonight."

"I didn't notice anything," Kim said tactfully.

"You must have!" Irma insisted. "They were like animated wax figures, and I'm sure wax figures could have offered a more stimulating conversation. When Johnny misbehaves, they just don't know what to do. So they freeze."

"The chill even reached me," Jim Blake said with a thin smile on his bony face.

"That contribution of yours about the monastery was a gem," Irma said with comic despair. "We'd have almost done better not to say anything." She turned to Kim. "What do you really think about us?"

"Nothing," she said. "I've been here only a short while. I hardly know any of you."

"That dinner must have seemed to last a thousand years," Irma said. "I know it did for me. We can blame Sheila for it all. She started Johnny drinking."

"No question of that," Jim Blake agreed.

Kim was curious. She said, "If I hadn't been here, if Johnny had returned home without me and gone to that cocktail party, what would have happened?"

Jim Blake nervously touched a finger to his small mustache. "Interesting speculation," he said.

Irma gave her a weary look. "I can tell you what would have happened. I've been through it all too many times before. Sheila would have welcomed him lovingly. Then, after a little, he would have teased her about her father's drinking or something else that annoys her, and they would have been at each other's throats even worse than tonight."

"Really?" Kim was astonished.

"Really," Irma said. "Sheila managed it rather differently tonight. She had her innings in a nice way and drove Johnny to drink. They've always had a pattern of battling and making up. It started when they were youngsters."

"So my being here didn't make all that much difference," Kim suggested.

"I'd say not," Irma replied. "Of course Sheila was upset to know that you and Johnny are thinking about marrying. But let me warn you—she won't give Johnny up easily."

"I gather that," Kim said with a wry smile.

"Depend on it," Irma told her. "She'll realize she made a bad move tonight. The next time she sees Johnny, there'll be no ghost talk. She'll be as sweet as sugar to him."

Jim Blake nodded. "I've seen her like that. Very deceptive girl. And always very jealous of Johnny even though they battle."

"I see that it's a complicated situation," Kim said.

"You can bet on that," Irma said. "I'm the rebel of the family and I like to speak frankly. I think Johnny is a rotten marriage bet. I can't understand how he managed to interest a nice girl like you!"

Kim knew she was blushing. "It's an unusual story," she told them.

"It would have to be," Irma said. "I can't imagine why Sheila is so much in love with him either. He's rarely faithful to any girl, and he has a cruel streak in him. If you haven't found that out, you will."

"I think I know what you mean," Kim said quietly.

Irma was studying her carefully. She said, "Whether you do or not, I can tell you that Sheila does. We grew up together, and he always had that bad strain in him. But you can't tell our father or mother that!"

Jim Blake gave Kim a knowing look. "Those two old people worship Johnny. To them he can do no wrong. That's why he is so spoiled."

"He's a very sensitive person," Kim said. "And he's working in a difficult profession."

Irma stared at her. "You'd understand that since you are an actress. That's the one good thing I can see in you two being engaged—you're both in the theater."

"That sometimes can be a problem," Kim said. "If you don't mind, I'm very tired. I think I'll go to bed early."

Irma smiled and went over and kissed her cheek. "I think we'll be great friends. Have a good night's sleep."

Jim Blake shook hands with her. "Nice knowing you, Kim."

As Kim started for the door Irma gave her a parting smile and she warned her, "Don't start seeing ghosts like Sheila!"

"I'll try not to," Kim said, feeling awkward. She turned and hurried out of the room and up the stairs. When she reached the big bedroom assigned to her, she went inside and closed the door with a feeling of escape.

From the moment she'd arrived at Craig House, it had been an ordeal. As a result, she was both physically and mentally weary. Kim quickly undressed and took a cold shower and then put on her nightgown. Before she got into bed she went over to the window and stared out. It was very peaceful outside, in contrast to the tensions among the people in the houses. Only the pleasant wash of the waves disturbed the quiet of the night.

In the distance she saw the beam of the Gull's Point Light. The island had a great deal of charm, and under other circumstances she was sure that she would enjoy it. But as it was, she had landed in the middle of a nightmare. It was too shattering!

Now she wondered why she had ever taken Johnny's offer seriously. She realized that it had largely been due to his charm. He had a way of making people do what he wished, and she had fallen victim to it. Whether she had to go back to hot New York and Gimbel's didn't matter. She surely couldn't live a summer with this tightly knit family group in which she was forced to lie. They would be bound to find out that her engagement to Johnny was only a pretense. The sooner she got away, the better.

While these things were going through her mind, her eyes settled on the cliffs. All at once she saw something which made her go tense and utter a tiny gasp. Down there in the shadows on the cliffs she was almost certain she saw the figure of a woman—the figure of a woman in a tightly fitted evening dress. She could not make out any details before the figure vanished. She had only the shadows left to stare at.

She was startled and tried to tell herself she was imagining things. But as she turned from the window, it remained in her mind to haunt her. She turned out the lights and slid between the cool sheets. Within a matter of minutes, she was deep in sleep.

It was not surprising that she dreamt, or that her dreams

were haunted by Johnny and a lovely girl in a shimmering dress wet with ocean water and tufted with strands of seaweed. They came hand in hand to stand before her—Johnny with a pleading look on his handsome face and the girl dull-eyed in the manner of the dead. Dull-eyed and pale as if she had been fished out of the water a corpse. And yet she stood there with Johnny!

Johnny whispered, "Touch her, Kim! Touch her!"

Kim was trembling, but she could not refuse him. Hesitantly she reached out with her hand to touch the flesh of the lovely dead girl. And when her fingers touched the flesh of the white arm the chill sent her staggering back with a cry of horror!

The cry of horror woke her up! She saw that she was in her bed in her room and there were no other figures alive or dead there. A gray dawn was beginning to show at the window. It would soon be morning. Her nightmare had been the result of her ordeal and Sheila's careless talk. With a sigh, she shut her eyes and went off to sleep again.

The island which she discovered when she rose the next morning was a very different one from the evening before. Everything was shrouded in fog. She was astounded at how quickly it had enveloped everything and how thick it was. She could barely see the cliffs and the evergreens which separated the Craig estate from the Moore property were lost in the gray mist.

She vaguely remembered her dream and reproached herself for giving way to such wild fancies. After she washed and dressed she went down to breakfast. She had no idea what time the rest of the family breakfasted, but it was nine o'clock and Irma was the only one at the table.

Johnny's sister smiled at her and said, "I hope you rested well."

"I did," she said, standing by the table.

"Sit anywhere," Irma said. "Everyone but Johnny has had breakfast. You look more rested."

"I feel fine," Kim said, taking a chair opposite the other girl.

Irma said, "You're getting a taste of our foggy weather."

"Yes. It came so fast."

"It goes the same way usually," Johnny's sister said, "though there are periods when we get thick fog for several days. It is dangerous driving; there always are several accidents, some of them bad ones. And boating is out of the question."

"Still, it keeps it cool," Kim said.

"That's true," Irma told her, rising. "If you don't mind, I'll leave you. I have a favorite television program to watch, women's lib type of talk show."

Kim smiled. "Sounds like fun."

Irma's pretty face took on one of her familiar grimaces. "I'd say diversion." And she left the room.

Kim was somewhat overwhelmed to have breakfast solemnly served to her by a uniformed maid. It was sheer grandeur compared to the usual way she lived. But even this affluent atmosphere was not going to tempt her. She decided that as soon as she met Johnny she would have a serious talk with him and make him see that it was best for her to leave.

Kim was finishing her coffee when Johnny came slowly into the long dining room. He had on slacks and a shirt open at the neck with a white sleeveless pullover over it. He looked shaken and pale.

"Good morning," she said.

"Good morning," he replied in a hollow voice. And then he added, "It really isn't. At least not for me!"

"I gather that by the way you look," she said. "Sit down and have some coffee."

"Thanks," he said, a grateful expression on his handsome face. "I have an idea I will be drinking lots of coffee this morning."

Kim poured him a cup of steaming black coffee from the silver pot the maid had left on the table for her. She waited until he had taken a few sips of it accompanied by deep sighs before she spoke again.

Then she said, "I lost you early last night."

He nodded, the coffee cup in hand. "Sorry about that."

"I wonder," she said. "I think you stood by that bar and got yourself deliberately drunk."

"Maybe."

Kim stared at him. "That is one thing predictable about you. You always take the easy way out."

Johnny frowned. "Don't start on me! Sheila did a good enough job last night!"

"It was silly of you to let her upset you."

"I didn't like her line of talk," he said sullenly.

She was studying him closely. "Why did you let that ghost talk upset you so?"

"Helen Walsh was my friend," he said grimly.

"But the poor girl is dead. Nothing Sheila says can hurt her now."

"I'm not thinking of that," Johnny said, a strange look on his face.

There was something in his tone that warned her. Something that was like a chill touch. In a small voice, she asked, "What do you mean?"

"I mean I don't think Helen Walsh drowned by accident," he said. "I think she was murdered!"

CHAPTER FIVE

The ashen-faced young man with the trembling hands seated across the table from Kim was a different Johnny Craig from the one she had known. As his words struck home to her, she realized that there was a good deal more to the situation in which she found herself than she had realized. Apparently he had other reasons for bringing her to Dark Harbor than fending off Sheila.

She stared at the young actor and in a tense voice said, "Are you really serious?"

"Yes." He looked more ill than ever.

"If you believe that, why haven't you done something about it?" she wanted to know. "It's not enough to get upset whenever her name is mentioned as you did last night."

Johnny put down his empty cup and stared at it miserably. "It's a long story. I don't want to discuss it here. We might be overheard."

"So?"

"When you've finished breakfast, we can go out for a walk," he said. "It's safer to talk outside."

"I'm not sure that sort of talk is safe anywhere," she said, with meaning.

Johnny summoned a weak smile and for a moment seemed at least a shadow of his regular self. "You proved yourself a good match for Sheila last night."

"I'm not so sure of that."

"She was almost hysterical with anger," he assured her. "I know her well enough to be able to tell. Of course, she covered it up well."

"I wonder what she'd think if she knew the truth," Kim suggested quietly.

Johnny raised his eyes quickly to meet hers. "She won't ever know the truth," he said.

"Maybe she should," Kim insisted.

He stood up. "It's nothing I want to discuss here. I'll see you outside." And he abruptly walked away from the table and out of the somber dining room.

Kim sat at the table for a few minutes after he left, thinking of what he had said. The big revelation had been his suggestion that Helen Walsh had met her death at the hands of a murderer rather than by accident. This was a frightening thought, and she was anxious to hear more about it, since Johnny was convinced that murder had taken place.

With a sigh she rose from the table and went upstairs to her room to wash and pick up her raincoat and a kerchief for her hair. The thick, damp fog would be almost as bad as rain for her hair, and she had an idea she might be outside for quite a long while. It would take Johnny Craig some time to explain the shocking possibility he'd brought up at the breakfast table.

She went downstairs and out the front door, but saw no sign of the handsome young actor. She then strolled across the lawn. The grass had been cut short, so she did not get her feet too wet. To the rear of the big mansion there was a wide patio area with all manner of lounges, easy chairs and tables with umbrellas for protection against sun and rain. And beyond the patio there was an area of grass in the center of which there was a good-sized kidney-shaped pool with lounges set out by it.

And standing beside the diving board staring into the turquoise depths of the pool's water was Johnny. He seemed so lost in his thoughts that he didn't see her. She walked over to where he stood and waited for him to speak first.

He finally glanced at her. "You did come!"

"Didn't you expect me?"

"I wasn't sure," he said. "You behaved sort of strangely at the table."

She arched an eyebrow. "Was that so surprising in view of what you said?"

"I suppose not," he said. Then he glanced around. "The place isn't so appealing when the fog is thick like this."

"Do you get this sort of fog often?"

"Often enough. It comes on fast and often vanishes just as quickly. I think this will burn off before the day is over."

"I suppose you get used to it and don't mind it," she said.

"I like the fog," he agreed. "And I like this pool area, though it is gloomy enough on a day like this."

"Pools can be rather sinister under certain conditions," she said. "Like deserted ponds in a deep woods. This pool has something of that air isolated as it is in this thick fog."

He said, "At least we can talk without being disturbed."

Kim sat on the rear area of the diving board. "You have a lot to explain."

Johnny's hands were in his pockets and he tried to project a nonchalant air. "Have I?"

"Yes," she said seriously, her eyes fixed on him. "I now begin to realize that you brought me down here under false pretenses. You didn't want me merely to protect you from a neurotic, lovesick Sheila. You had some other game you planned to play. And if you expect me to remain here, you'd better tell me honestly about it now."

"Is that an ultimatum?"

"It is," she said firmly.

He studied her as if to be sure that she meant what she had said. Evidently he decided that she had. He took his hands from his pockets and sat down on the damp diving board beside her. For a moment he said nothing, just stared off into the thick gray mist.

At last he told her. "All right. I *did* bring you down here for more than one reason."

"Go on."

"I hoped that in addition to protecting me from Sheila's romantic notions, you might also be a means of my discovering whether Helen Walsh was murdered or not."

She frowned. "Can you explain that?"

"Easy," he said. "I think that the same person who caused Helen's death might also cause yours."

Kim was silent for a few seconds and then, in a carefully controlled voice, she said, "Of course the person you suspect is Sheila."

His eyes met hers. "I'm glad you guessed for yourself."

"It wasn't all that hard," she said bitterly.

He sighed. "My idea is that Sheila became wildly jealous of Helen and shoved her off that pleasure boat when Helen was too drunk to save herself. I think Sheila will also try to get rid of you some way if she thinks I'm going to marry you."

"Which rumor you've been careful to spread," Kim said sarcastically.

"I had to bait a trap for her," Johnny said.

"The fact that you are placing me in great danger hasn't bothered you at all, has it?" Kim exclaimed in an outraged tone.

Johnny looked uncomfortable. "I planned to keep a close eye on you. Protect you from her!"

"You were in fine shape to protect me last night," she said in bitter accusation.

"I'm sorry about that."

"You ought to be," she said. "I don't know what to think.

You're telling me that Sheila is a psychotic—dangerous enough to have murdered someone."

"Yes."

Kim gave a deep sigh. "You may be interested to hear that she did some talking to me about your failings last night. What she said added up to a rather frightening portrait."

Johnny showed annoyance. "What did she say about me?"

"I'm not sure I should tell you," Kim said.

Johnny said, "You don't have to. I think I know. She likely went back to when we were kids and that pet cat of hers was hanged."

Kim was surprised that he should come up with this so easily. She stared at him doubtfully. "You recalled *that* soon enough."

"She's told that story on me before," he said in a grim tone. "She has never forgiven me—and I had nothing to do with it!"

"She thinks so. She firmly believes that you killed her pet to even a score with her."

Johnny said, "She ought to know better. There was someone else around whom I'm almost certain did it. I was not involved."

"Who else?"

"Someone not around now."

"Can't you say who? Mention a name?"

"I'd rather not," the young actor said unhappily.

"That isn't very satisfactory," she told him. "This other party who is supposed to be guilty could well not exist at all. You may have made them up to exonerate yourself."

He stared at her. "You think that?"

"I don't know what to think anymore," she said. "You brought me here under false pretenses, and now you are placing me in danger of my life."

"You're making too much of that," he protested.

"Not from my viewpoint," she said. "So you didn't hang Sheila's cat! Wouldn't she have some idea who else might be guilty?"

"She would if she were fair."

"You think she isn't fair?"

"I do," Johnny said. "Because of my father and mother, and the family generally, I don't want to go into this any further. But I wasn't guilty."

Kim shot him a knowing glance. "Irma doesn't see you as a good marriage risk, either. She warned me against you last night."

"That sounds like Irma," he said wryly.

"At least she's an honest person!"

"You think so?"

"Yes."

"And I suppose you like that boyfriend of hers, Jim Blake?" he asked in an angry tone.

"I don't know that much about him," she said.

"Better if you let it remain that way," Johnny said. "And as far as Sheila's stories about me are concerned, they have no more substance than all the other things she imagines."

The thick mist was more like rain than fog. In the distance she heard the bleak sound of a foghorn. She gave Johnny a sharp glance. "Sheila spoke of something else—of a girl who fell into a gravel pit and was killed. What about that?"

He shook his head. "So she brought that up, too?"

"Yes."

"She was really trying to do me in," Johnny said grimly. "All that happened years ago. When I was around twelve or so!"

"She claimed you resented some little girl who used to

play with your crowd. According to her, you were alone with the girl when she had her fatal accident and the circumstances were suspicious."

"Only to Sheila," be exclaimed. "Only in her twisted mind! Don't you see she was merely trying to frighten you? Turn you against me?"

"But the accident did happen?"

"I can't deny that."

"So it could have been as she said?"

"But it wasn't," he protested. "Ask old Dr. Taylor—he was the first to arrive and try and save that girl's life. He'll tell you it was an accident."

"I want to believe that it was," Kim said solemnly.

"Then do! What Sheila was trying to imply about me is all too true about her. She's trying to depict me as a murderer when *she* is the one who has killed."

She stared at him hard. "I wonder. There are other things, Johnny. Things which have happened in the last few years. Accidents which are sometimes hard to account for."

"I swear I've never deliberately harmed anyone," Johnny protested. He was so boyishly appealing in his declaration that Kim found it hard to doubt him.

But there had been the incident of her scalded hand. She had never been able to make her mind up about that. Then there had been the time Babs Darriot had taken the bad fall. Johnny had either accidentally stumbled against the old actress or deliberately shoved her. Again it was hard to be certain which had happened. And the cruel accidents which had occurred to his other girlfriends and which had been noted in the press. Had all these things been purely coincidental?

She studied him with anxious eyes. "I worry that you are always acting," she said. "I'm not sure I know when to believe you."

"Believe me now," he urged her and he placed one of his tanned, strong hands on hers.

The hand was a reminder of how cruel his grip could be when he liked. She tried to shut the memory of this from her mind. And she went on to ask him, "You say that Sheila may have murdered this Helen Walsh? Tell me more about it."

He wrinkled his brow. "You've already heard something about Helen. That she was a popular sort of good-time girl."

"A girl who worked in a shop in Dark Harbor and liked to go to parties."

"And she wasn't particular with whom she went or with whom she had an affair," Johnny said grimly. "She knew her good looks were her chief asset and she put them to the best possible use."

"You and she were close friends?"

"Sure," the young actor said. "But she was friendly with a lot of other people."

"Like whom?"

"Like the wonderful Jim Blake for instance," Johnny said with grim satisfaction. "Before my father hired him as the family lawyer and he became interested in Irma, he went around with Helen a lot."

"I see," she said. "But at the time of this pleasure boat cruise, you were playing Helen against Sheila?"

He looked guilty. "Why do you say that?"

"It fits your thinking," she said. "You brought me down here to play against Sheila. You seem to enjoy tormenting her because she is unfortunate enough to have a crush on you."

"It's more than a crush," he grumbled. "She's trying to get me to marry her."

"Tell me more about Helen."

He hesitated and then said, "So I was seeing a lot of her. Sheila and I had one of our rows and I wasn't dating her.

Helen didn't ask anything from me but my company. We had some good times together."

"Did you really care for her?"

"Maybe."

"And she never mentioned marriage to you?" Kim asked him.

"No strings," he said. "That's one of the things I liked about her most. Helen enjoyed the fun of our relationship, and she didn't ask anything beyond that."

Somewhat bitterly, Kim said, "Because you had the advantage of her. She knew her low social status and tarnished reputation didn't give her any bargaining angle. You had it all your own way."

"Now you're being unfair," he protested. "I didn't feel that way about Helen. I respected her."

"I hope so," she said. "I never met the girl, but I find myself beginning to feel sorry for her."

"You needn't. Helen could look after herself."

"I'm not convinced," Kim said. "I have an idea she must at least have had some hopes about you. It wouldn't have been normal for her not to have. But to you she was just a safe, easy playmate!"

"I took her to all the parties," he protested.

"And she was drinking heavily," Kim reminded him. "I find that girls in a spot like Helen's often drink a lot to try and ease their pain."

"You're being melodramatic!"

"I'm trying to reconstruct things. I'd say that Helen was probably deeply in love with you. That may be why Sheila became so desperate. She saw the danger and the possibility even if you didn't. She pictured you marrying Helen without even thinking too much about it."

Johnny looked sheepish. "You really believe that?"

"Yes," she said. "What about the night of Helen's death?"

"We were out on a cruise in a boat owned by a friend of mine. About forty of us. I brought Helen along as my date."

"Who brought Sheila?"

"Jim Blake."

Kim showed surprise. "Jim Blake? But didn't he bring Irma?"

"Irma had a sick headache and didn't want to go. Sheila found out and asked Jim to take her. Nothing devious, just a simple arrangement between friends."

"I see."

Johnny recalled, "They had a musician aboard playing an accordion. I paid him to play some of my favorite tunes. Somehow late in the evening I became separated from Helen."

"And?"

"Around one o'clock I met Jim Blake in the cabin and I asked him where Sheila was. He said the last he'd seen of her she was talking with Helen on the aft deck."

"What then?"

"I went in search of Helen and couldn't find her," the young man said in a troubled voice. "I found myself getting edgy. Then I ran into Sheila and she seemed in a kind of a strange, exhilarated mood. Yet she hadn't been drinking that much. I asked her about Helen."

"What did she say?"

"She denied having seen her. I quoted Jim Blake and she shrugged and said maybe she'd spoken to her in passing. But I couldn't get any admission that they'd had a long talk or that she knew where Helen was."

"But Helen was missing?"

"Yes," he sighed. "I went to the fellow who owned the boat and we made a thorough search. She wasn't anywhere to be found and we were a couple of miles out at sea. It meant only one thing—she had gone over the side."

"Then what did you do?"

"The boat owner sent out an emergency call to the Coast Guard. There was always a small chance she might have managed to keep afloat for a while or that another boat had found her. We headed for Dark Harbor at once. No one felt in a party mood any longer."

"But she was never found?"

"Never," Johnny said ruefully. "And I noticed that Sheila kept nicely in the background when the police questioned the members of the party. It was then I decided that she was the one who'd shoved Helen overboard."

"But you didn't tell anyone?"

"No," he said. "I had no way of proving it."

"So you kept this to yourself?"

"You're the first I've told because I needed to tell somebody. I was sure you'd see things as I do."

"I'm not certain of that," she said slowly.

"Sheila started this ghost thing because the murder is on her mind," he went on. "I say she's mad. And I thought with someone I could trust here to help me I might trap her into a confession."

Kim stared at him. "It's quite a story."

"No one has ever seen Helen's ghost except Sheila," Johnny went on. "No one ever will. The ghost is a figment of Sheila's imagination."

"She made it sound real enough to me."

"I know," he admitted.

She gave a tiny shudder. "The whole thing frightens me. It is more than I bargained for. I still say I should go back to the mainland."

Johnny protested. "You told me you'd work for me for the summer."

She said, "You didn't tell me all the terms of the job."

"I was afraid to."

She said, "It may surprise you to know that if I do stay on, it is because of Helen Walsh."

His eyebrows raised. "Because of Helen?"

She nodded. "Yes. I feel a deep sympathy for her."

"You never knew her."

"That doesn't matter," Kim said. "I don't think anyone had the right to murder her and get away with it."

"Nor do I," the young actor said.

"The police don't suspect Sheila?"

"How could they?" he asked. "They don't know what we do."

"You should have discussed it with them."

"That would only have alerted Sheila to my suspicions, and then there never would be any hope of trapping her."

Kim listened with a growing feeling that she might have been unfair to Johnny. She had lined up with the critics of the young playboy actor. It could be that he was being entirely truthful and that he was really trying to avenge Helen Walsh's murder, if it were a murder.

She got up from the diving board and turned facing him. "How can you be sure it was a murder? Helen may have become tipsy and ill and fallen overboard."

"I'd think that if Sheila hadn't started this business of her seeing Helen's ghost. That is what convinced me she is somehow guilty."

"Maybe," she said.

Johnny also rose from the divine board. "You will stay?"

"I'll make no long-time promises," she said. "I'll stay for a while."

"Thanks," he said, looking a little brighter. "Just hearing you say that makes me feel better. I was afraid last night might have finished you, that you'd refuse to stay on."

"Perhaps I should," she said with a sigh. "But I won't."

These words exactly described her state of mind. She was confused and a little frightened. Once again she felt like a late recruit in a drama in which the plot wasn't clear to her. The luxury of her surroundings at Craig House should have put her at ease. Instead she felt extremely tense. There were things that puzzled her and she had an idea Johnny's family resented her in spite of their seemingly, warm welcome.

At lunch it struck her this was borne out. Madeline and Stephen Craig barely talked to her. The few words they exchanged were with each other and had to do with a discussion concerning the annual church sale. Johnny's mother contended the sale should go on twice during the summer while her husband insisted once was plenty. It appeared to be a source of contention between them which had existed for a long while.

Irma in a black-and-white checked sports jacket was her usual attractive but acid self. She told Kim, "I saw you and Johnny down by the pool this morning. You seemed to be there for hours."

Johnny had left the table after eating only his salad and downing a glass of milk. This left Kim on her own to reply to his sister.

Kim said, "Yes. We did talk a long while."

Irma smiled knowingly. "Lovers dote on being in each other's company! But I can think of more comfortable places to hold a rendezvous than by the pool on a bleak morning like this."

Kim said, "I don't think we were much aware of where we were."

"Your conversation must have really been something!" Irma said.

Kim resented this fishing for information on the part of Johnny's sister. She said rather pertly, "Well, as you say, lovers will talk for ages about anything!" And she excused herself politely and left the table.

She had no idea where Johnny had gone and she had no desire to spend time talking to his sister after the exchange at the luncheon table. She simply wanted to be by herself for a little and sort out her thoughts. She also wanted to write a letter to Bill Griffith, though she didn't know how much she dare put in her message to him.

Upstairs in her room, there was a small desk and chair and she found a supply of paper and envelopes in it. The Craigs knew how to take care of their guest's needs. She sat down at the desk and began the letter to Bill. She wrote more than she had intended and it took quite a while.

By the time she finished, she saw from her window that the fog had almost miraculously vanished. It was sunny again and it looked very pleasant out. She decided that she would ask for permission to use the Mercedes or some other utility vehicle and drive into town with her letter and mail it. She was tense about remaining at the old mansion all the time, and she wanted to see the town at her leisure.

Sealing the letter, she rose and prepared to leave. She took in the details of her large room. Its windows overlooking the ocean provided a wonderful panoramic view and the fireplace at one end of the room was of beach stone and seemed to be practical. The furniture was all of rustic maple and suited the atmosphere of the old country house. She had her modern bathroom, likely a new addition, and two huge walk-in closets. There was also another door, which could lead to a third closet. She wasn't sure because it was locked. The walls of the room were papered in a rich brown pattern of leaves entwined in a design and the woodwork was of light oak. The house must have been expensive to build in its day, and by modern standards it was a spacious palace.

She went downstairs to ask about getting a car and was surprised to find herself confronting Johnny's mother and Sheila Moore!

Sheila, vibrant in a red suit with golden buttons and belt, and a golden shirt open at the neck, smiled warmly at Kim as soon as she saw her. "Hi!" Sheila said. "I wondered where you were hiding!"

"I wasn't hiding," Kim replied. "I was writing a letter and I thought I'd go to Dark Harbor and mail it."

Madeline Craig's pale face showed mild disapproval of this plan. She said, "No need to go to the village. The postman will take your letters to mail when he comes by with our mail tomorrow. He does it all the time for us."

Kim said, "I'd prefer to mail it myself. I'd like to see more of Dark Harbor."

"Oh!" Madeline Craig said vaguely.

Sheila seized on this at once. "You are so right," she enthused. "Half the fun of coming here for the summer is the quaintness of the place. I feel it, and I've been used to it since I was a child."

"It has changed so," Madeline Craig lamented.

"Not all that much," Sheila said. "I'm driving into Dark Harbor. Why don't you come with me?"

Kim's first reaction was to refuse. Then she realized that it was important that she get to know Sheila better. It was her whole reason for being there. She had to find out about the girl for herself, not merely take Johnny's word about her.

Kim said, "I wonder where Johnny is."

Madeline Craig promptly supplied the information. "Sheila just asked me the same question. He has gone to play golf with his father."

"Oh," she said. She thought Johnny might have told her.

"I'm driving into town alone," Sheila said. "My car is outside."

"I'll have to get back," Kim said, hesitating. "You may be in a hurry."

Sheila's green eyes were flecked with mischief. She said, "Not at all. I can make my return drive to suit you."

"Very well," Kim said, since there was little else she could do but accept.

They left Mrs. Craig in the shadowed hallway and went out into the bright sunlight. Sheila had a foreign car with a sliding panel for a sun roof. The panel was open now, and both girls sat in the front seat.

Kim said, "I like your car."

"Thanks," Sheila said. "I enjoy a good car, and this one is very easy on gas as well."

Kim settled back as Sheila started the car and drove out along the narrow roadway which led to the main road. As an opener, she said, "I enjoyed your party last night."

"I'm surprised to hear you say that," Sheila said, her eyes on the road. She was wearing large dark sunglasses now which hid a good deal of her facial expression.

"Why?"

"Johnny left in high dudgeon and took you with him. My mention of the ghost seemed to do it."

"Yes," Kim said. "I notice he is ultrasensitive on that subject." She decided to keep up a discussion of the ghost if possible and find out Sheila's reaction now that Johnny wasn't there to be taunted.

Sheila glanced at her from the wheel as she halted the car before moving out onto the main highway. She said, "I'm glad you said 'ultrasensitive.' I think that is a good description of his behavior."

"If you know he resents talk of the ghost, why do you bring it up?" Kim asked with supposed innocence.

Sheila kept her eyes on the wheel. "Maybe I enjoy tormenting him. He likes to torment everyone else."

"You think so?"

"I know it," Sheila said. "And so should you by now. He was cruel enough to Helen Walsh when she was alive."

"He tells me they had wonderful times together."

"I'm sure of it," Sheila said scornfully. "But you can be sure she made all the sacrifices. Johnny is a selfish devil."

"Most men are."

"Johnny is something else again," Sheila said. "You know, he promised to marry me."

"Did he really?" Kim tried hard to sound casual.

"Then he shows up here with you as his intended bride," the girl at the wheel said angrily.

Kim said, "After all the things you told me about him last night, I'm surprised that you would ever consider marrying him. You claimed his cruelty began as a child."

"It did," Sheila said bitterly. "He was cruel then and he hasn't changed any. But I happen to be fool enough to still care for him."

"It's too bad he doesn't feel the same way about you," Kim said. "You might make an excellent couple."

Sheila smiled thinly. "You're being most generous."

"I mean it. I'm not all that sure that Johnny and I ever will marry. We could be just a temporary thing."

"I'm counting on that," the girl at the wheel said frankly. "I think he brought you down here to make me come to his terms."

"His terms?"

"Yes."

"I don't understand."

"You should," Sheila said. "When any marriage is being planned, each person has to set out his own ideas and plans for the future. Johnny knows that I have some different ambitions from him, and he wants to bend me to his wishes before he'll agree to marry me. So he's using you to whip me into submission."

Kim listened to this with some skepticism. It didn't fit what Johnny had told her. But it did go along with the obsession which Sheila seemed to have for him.

Kim said, "That's why you were so abrasive last night. You resented his latest attempt to bring you into line."

"Call it that," Sheila said.

"I think you're wrong," Kim told her quietly. "I'm sure if I want to I can marry Johnny."

"You think so?" Sheila asked in a hostile, icy voice.

"Yes," Kim said. "I see we're in the town. I hardly noticed with us having such an interesting talk."

Sheila slowed the car down as they headed along a side street with a number of tiny shops in newly shingled cottages. She nodded at a cottage on the left and said, "That's the boutique where Helen Walsh was a clerk. She also thought she could marry Johnny. And look where she is now!"

CHAPTER SIX

It seemed to Kim that the black-haired girl's comment was close to being a threat. Nevertheless, she chose to ignore it and said nothing as they drove onto the hilly Main Street. When they reached the red brick one-story building which housed the post office, Sheila let her out.

"Suppose I meet you back here in a half-hour," Sheila suggested.

"Thank you," Kim said. "As long as that is convenient for you."

"It will suit me fine," Sheila said and she drove off up the hill.

Kim posted her letter and then left the post office to stroll down the steep hill which led to the wharves. She passed by the Green Heron Lounge and Hotel and then halted to gaze in the window of a gift shop which dealt chiefly in fine chinaware.

"Thinking of making a purchase?" a hearty male voice said behind her. Kim turned quickly and saw Dr. Henry Taylor, the elderly doctor whom she'd met at the cocktail party the previous night.

"You're Dr. Taylor!"

"The same," he agreed with a chuckle. "I've been making a few house calls down here. I expect I'm about the last doctor on the Cape to make them."

"I think there are times when house calls are needed," she said.

The white-haired man with the horn-rimmed glasses

nodded in agreement. "Especially when people are very ill or very old. I pick my cases."

"Of course that's sensible," she said.

"Where is Johnny this afternoon?" the doctor asked.

She smiled. "He's gone off to play golf with his father."

"And left you on your own?" Dr. Taylor sounded surprised.

"Sheila drove me in. I wanted to take a look around the town by myself."

"Good idea," Dr. Taylor said. "You'll find plenty of things to interest you. The island has a long history."

"So I've been told."

"And the Craig family has played a major role in the island story," he said. "Are you impressed by that old house?"

"I couldn't help but be impressed," she said.

"I know," he agreed. "A good number of Craigs have lived and died there. Drop by my office some day and see my miniature hospital wing."

"I want to," she said. "People have told me about it and the fine work you are doing."

"I wouldn't say it's anything special," the white-haired man said modestly. "I'm just a country doctor on an island. My patients are more confined than if they were on the mainland. So I have to give them my best."

"I'm sure you'd do that wherever you might be," she said.

Dr. Taylor smiled. "If you have any problems I may be able to help you with, don't hesitate to call on me."

"I won't," she said.

"I think you've done a lot for Johnny," the doctor told her. "He used to be much more nervous than he seems now. I'm glad there's a change in him."

They chatted a few minutes longer and then they each went their separate ways, the doctor heading for his parked car and Kim walking on down to the wharves. Kim stood on the ferry wharf and watched the pleasure craft in the harbor for a while. It was a constantly changing scene, the sleek white hulls of motor craft mixing with the colorful sails of the sailing boats. Before she knew it she had to rush back to the post office and meet Sheila.

The black-haired girl was parked there waiting for her. When Kim got in the car, Sheila said, "Did you get all your errands done?"

"Yes," Kim said. "Then I walked as far as the wharves and I saw Dr. Taylor."

"He's a real relic of the island," Sheila said as she started the car.

"A lively relic. He's a very nice man."

Sheila sighed. "I suppose so. In the old days he was sort of a father image to me. But I don't see much of him now. You don't live with your family, do you?"

"No," Kim said, without going into any details about what remained of her family. "I live in New York. I share an apartment with another girl."

Sheila made a face. "That sounds great. I live with my father! Can you imagine that?"

"It doesn't sound so bad," she said.

"You don't know my father," Sheila said, her eyes fixed on the road ahead. "If he were a poor man, he'd be the island drunk. Because he has plenty of money, he's considered a heavy social drinker. Or, to quote the whispers, he's a bad alcoholic."

Once again Kim found herself feeling sympathy for Sheila in spite of all she'd heard. She said, "I'm sorry."

"You sound as if you mean it," Sheila said bitterly.

"I do."

"Thanks. It isn't much fun. He wasn't around last night.

Up in his room dead drunk. But you'll see him around one of these days. He manages to sober up a little now and then."

"Isn't there anything that can be done to help him?"

"We've tried the whole strata of cures. None of them worked. The point is that he doesn't want them to work. He enjoys this special misery of his."

"At least you sound as if you understand him," she said.

"I do," Sheila agreed. "But I don't manage him too well. I'm impatient when it comes to drunks."

"Most people are," Kim said.

Sheila slowed the car and they turned into the narrower road which led to the Craig house. Sheila said, "We made good time getting there and back."

"I agree," Kim said.

"Did you have a good chat with the doctor?" Sheila wanted to know.

"Yes," she said.

"He can tell you about all of us," Sheila said with a look of thoughtfulness on her pretty face. "Do you want me to show you where I've seen the ghost?"

Kim said, "I would guess right out there along the edge of the cliffs."

The other girl showed amazement. "That *is* one of the spots! How did you know?"

Kim watched Sheila carefully to see what her reaction would be as she told her, "I think I may have seen the ghost last night."

Sheila looked thunderstruck. "You're joking!"

"Why should I be?" she asked.

Sheila looked uncomfortable as she said, "I don't know. I thought I was the only one who ever sees that ghost! At least up until now, I'm the only one who has admitted to seeing her."

"Do you expect her to remain your personal phantom?" Kim asked.

The black-haired girl looked flustered. "Hardly! I mean it's just such a surprise for someone else to tell me they've seen the phantom."

"I saw *something*," Kim said. "It was too dark and the figure much too blurred to be certain about it."

"Frightening!" Sheila exclaimed.

"Not to me," Kim said, getting out of the car.

"You didn't ever meet her when she was alive," Sheila said. "That's bound to make a difference."

"What difference does it make?"

"I mean, it isn't so macabre for you. The sight of her makes my flesh creep. Maybe you won't mind her showing herself here."

"Perhaps not."

Sheila stared at her. She had remained seated behind the wheel of the car for all this. Now, through the window, she said, "I think you're probably bluffing me anyhow."

Kim smiled coolly. "You mean in return for your wild line of ghost talk last night?"

"Could be!" Sheila said and she started the car and drove off.

Kim felt the exchange with the black-haired girl had been a somewhat revealing one. Sheila had immediately doubted that she had ever seen the ghost. And Kim felt this was because the ghostly appearances were a figment of Sheila's imagination. Perhaps the imagining of a guilty mind, if Johnny's story about that night on the boat were true.

Kim had not lied when she claimed she'd seen a mysterious figure walking along the cliffs. But she well knew the figure could have been anyone. It had been too far away for her to make out details. She had purposely linked the incident with the ghost to try Sheila, and Sheila had not handled it too well.

She went upstairs and was about to enter her room when she saw Johnny's mother coming along the hall. She noted the white-haired woman's wraithlike manner as she approached and realized that Madeline Craig seemed to be continually nervous.

The older woman halted to ask her, "Did you have a pleasant drive?"

"Yes. It was very nice in Dark Harbor," she replied.

"I'm glad the fog went out," Madeline Craig said. "How do you like your room?"

"Very much," Kim said. "The closets are wonderful. And there is one door that is locked, I assume it is another closet, and I certainly don't need it."

The older woman seemed to become more tense. "That door leads to the room adjoining yours. We haven't used the room for years, so we always keep it locked."

"Really? I would expect it would have an excellent view. Mine has," Kim said.

"We prefer not to use that room," Madeline Craig said coldly, without offering any explanation.

"I see. I don't suppose Johnny has returned yet?"

"Not yet," his mother said and glided off in the direction of the stairway.

Kim went on into her room, puzzled by the woman's strange attitude about the room next to hers. The locked room! Madeline Craig always gave the impression of someone with a dark secret, and her behavior in this instance was doubly suspicious. Kim eyed the door and then went over and tried the handle again. It would not turn. And when she bent down to peek through the keyhole, she was frustrated to find that it had been stuffed with something on the other side.

TERROR AT DARK HARBOR

A mystery room! And located directly adjoining the one she had been given. It made her wonder whether there was anything sinister about the room and why she had been placed in the room next to it. She made up her mind to try and get some more word about the room. But she knew it would be useless to ask Johnny or any of the other Craigs. They seemed to enjoy keeping her in the dark about everything that was happening.

She rested until it was time to ready herself for dinner. She had just washed and dressed when there was a light knock on her door. When she opened it, Johnny was standing there. He had changed into a white sports jacket and blue trousers and was wearing a blue shirt and white tie.

"You're finally home," she said.

"Yes. May I come in?" he asked.

"Of course," she said, opening the door wider.

He gave her a look. "I hear you were in Dark Harbor when I was gone."

"Yes."

He kept staring at her. "Sheila drove you."

"She did."

"I'd prefer it if you didn't make friends with her."

Her eyes widened. "You didn't tell me that!"

"I thought you'd understand, especially since I've told you the real reason I've had you come here."

"Now just a minute," she protested. "You can't expect me to live by a lot of rules—especially when you're not around to consult."

"I should have seen you before I left," he apologized.

"And if I don't associate with Sheila, how am I going to discover anything about her?" Kim wanted to know.

"She's around. You're bound to see a lot of her."

She gave him a bitter smile. "Are you afraid she'll corrupt

me? Tell me some story that doesn't fit with yours?"

The handsome young actor clenched his hands and his face crimsoned. He said, "I don't think that's funny!"

"Sorry!"

"You are here as my employee, need I remind you?" His tone was stern.

"It's a bad arrangement. I think I should end it."

Johnny became less arrogant. Raising a hand, he said wearily, "Don't get me wrong! I don't want a quarrel about this. The truth is I was worried about you—worried that Sheila might worm too much information out of you."

"That's hardly likely," Kim said.

Johnny came close to her. "Let's just forget it!" His eyes were tenderly admiring. "You look lovely tonight." He took her in his arms and kissed her.

Kim was ready to ask him if he expected the kisses to be part of her employment, but decided against it. She accepted the kiss for what it seemed to be, a genuine tribute to her. She liked many things about Johnny Craig and wished that he would not continually confuse her by presenting so many different faces.

Downstairs dinner was another sober ordeal. When they finished, Johnny suggested they go for a drive and she agreed. He took her out along the shore road to the large estate still known as the monastery. He parked his car along the road by it so she could get a good look at it.

"You say that it was once a leper hospital?" she asked him.

"Operated by the monks for years."

"And now it's privately owned?"

"Yes, though I understand it is available for sale," Johnny said.

"I don't think I'd like to live there," was her comment. "It has a kind of sinister look and it is located a long distance from the majority of houses on the island."

"You're probably right," he said. "The location is a little lonely."

He started the car again and they drove back to the more populated area of the island. He found a parking place by a small park near the Dark Harbor Museum. In a tiny white bandstand in the middle of the green expanse of park, a band was playing. It was a small band—perhaps ten instruments—but it sounded good in the twilight of this pleasant summer evening.

"Is that a local band?" she asked.

"Yes," he said. "It's made up of members of the volunteer fire department. You see, our island has everything."

She laughed. "I'm beginning to believe it."

"I came here often when I was a youngster," Johnny said. "We boys used to sit on the grass and drink beer. We kept out of sight of our elders, of course."

Kim glanced up at his smiling face. "You really had good times here on the island, didn't you?"

"The best I've ever known," he said with deep sincerity.

They strolled around the park where a lot of people had gathered. There were a few light green benches for the older folk, but mostly people either walked about or sat on the grass.

Johnny suddenly said, "There's a fellow over there I want to speak to for a moment. He's a boat builder, and he's supposed to have a small boat finished for Irma. I want to ask him when it will be done. Will you excuse me?"

"Of course," she said.

He walked away in the growing darkness and she saw him go up to a stout middle-aged man who'd been standing listening to the concert with two other men. The lights which rimmed the grandstand had gone on and also strings of lights which ran between telephone poles at the edge of one side of the park. The music continued and the tiny park had more glamour under the colored lights and the stars.

"Good evening, Miss Rice," a rasping male voice said and she turned to see an elderly man in a dark blue suit and white cap with a black peak. She immediately recognized him as Captain Zachary Miller, whom she'd met on the wharf.

"You're Captain Miller," she said, happy that she'd been able to remember his name.

"That's right," he agreed with a chuckle. He had a good-looking face for an old man, despite his many wrinkles and his weathered skin. He was leaning on a gnarled cane as he stood with her.

"Johnny has gone over to speak with some boat builder," she explained.

The old man nodded. "Mack Carter," he said. "I see them over there. Mack is long-winded. Count on him keeping Johnny a long while."

"It has something to do with a boat he hasn't delivered."

"That would be Mack—never gets anything done on time. He's not like his father and grandfather. His grandfather had one of the most successful boat-building outfits on the island but now it's all run down. Mack is plain lazy."

"How unfortunate," she said.

"Happens," the old captain said. "How do you like the concert?"

"It's a nice surprise. I had no idea there was anything like this on the island."

"We do pretty well by ourselves. Of course, the great days are over. They ended when whaling was finished."

Kim said, "I think you have a fine future catering to tourists since the island is so interesting."

He nodded. "Long as they don't spoil it. They have a way of coming in and buying up and then overdeveloping."

"I know what you mean," she said. "The Cape is like that."

"Not too many families like the Craigs still living in the houses built by their forebears," the old captain said. "A lot of the properties have changed hands."

"I suppose so," she said. "Johnny seems to like the island."

Captain Miller nodded. "I remember him here as a boy. A wild young fellow, but likable. Now I hear he's a big movie star."

"He has been quite successful," she agreed.

"You like Craig House?" the old man asked.

"It's a wonderful old place," she said. "There are some lovely pines between it and the Moore place."

"I know about them," Captain Miller said. "They're Japanese black pines. Johnny's grandfather planted them around 1895. They are the tallest trees on the island and they do well because the conditions here are similar to the sea winds and water off the coast of Japan."

"That's interesting," she said. "I knew they were different."

"We have a lot of Scotch and white pine on the island," Captain Miller went on. "And they do pretty well, too." He paused a moment and then asked, "Is Johnny's Aunt Grace still around?"

"I don't know," she said. "I don't think so."

"You'd know if she was," the old man said. "She was an older sister of his father's. Always a kind of shy girl. She had a nervous breakdown when she was in her twenties. I don't know the rights of it. But I hear she was violent and they had to put her in a mental hospital."

"Oh?"

"Tried to kill her younger sister, so the story goes. That

was Nell. She's dead now. There was only Stephen and Grace Craig left. She wasn't ever completely cured, but she was well enough to come here summers."

Kim said, "You mean they brought her here to Craig House to live?"

"That's right. About twenty years after it all happened, they began to bring her here for the holidays. No one ever saw her except when she got off the ferry and got on again. Then she was always with Stephen and his wife and they didn't encourage anyone to speak with her."

"A strange situation."

"It was," the old man agreed. "I knew Grace, but I didn't feel like calling by to see her since I was afraid she mightn't know me and it might even upset her. I saw her once from a distance after they started bringing her back here. She had faded a lot and she seemed stooped. That puzzled me since she wasn't that old."

"A tragedy for her," Kim said.

"It was. And she was a nice girl. But then there has always been a streak of insanity in the Craig family," Captain Miller said.

Kim heard these words with a feeling of uneasiness. "You mean she wasn't the first in the family to show signs of insanity?"

"No," the old man said. "There was a young Craig years before her who went mad. He drowned off Gull Point one night, which was probably a good thing. He was dangerous enough to be locked up then."

She was thinking of Johnny and his strangeness. She couldn't help but worry that the strain of madness might have reappeared in the family in another generation. She asked the old captain, "Do you really think families pass on a strain of madness?"

"Yes," he said. "I guess it's like any other physical trait."

She said, "You mean like facial features, the color of eyes and hair, birthmarks, and that sort of thing you see repeated in families."

"That's right," the old captain agreed. "Madness is much the same. I could name three or four island families with an inherited tendency to madness."

Kim said, "I must ask Johnny about his Aunt Grace. But I'm sure she can't be here this summer or I surely would have seen her."

"I'd expect so," Captain Miller said. "Chances are she has become worse so that they can't have her here, or maybe she has died. She'd have to be seventy if she were alive."

She said, "Stephen Craig seems almost that old himself. But then he and his wife are very mature types."

The old captain chuckled. " 'Mature' hardly covers it. They are the most conservative couple on the island. Stephen would be about two years younger than Grace if she is still alive."

"Did they have a nurse or companion for Grace?"

"I think Madeline cared for her mostly," the old man said. "Of course, she couldn't be allowed to leave the house alone. That was one of the considerations understood when the hospital allowed her to come here in their custody."

"They would have to keep a close watch on her since she had been dangerous," Kim agreed.

Johnny came strolling back, and this ended their discussion. The old captain moved on while she and Johnny remained to listen to the music for a little longer. The concert ended and they went back to the car to return to Craig House. It wasn't until they were driving back that she asked him about his Aunt Grace.

His first reaction was one of annoyance. This did not at all surprise her since she was used to his quick temper. He asked her, "Who told you about Aunt Grace?"

"Captain Miller," she said.

"Trust that old fossil to keep up gossip," the actor said. "So that is what he was talking to you about."

"That and a lot of other things. I was interested in hearing about your aunt, and I wondered what might have happened to her."

At the wheel in the darkness, Johnny kept grimly studying the road ahead. "Aunt Grace is dead."

"Oh?"

"She's been dead for several years."

"The captain said he knew her."

"Probably," Johnny agreed. "But he couldn't have talked with her for years. When my mother and father brought her here, she lived as a recluse."

"Did she live in the main house?"

"Yes, in the room next to yours."

This came as a shock. Kim exploded: "The locked room!"

Johnny gave her a quick side-glance. "How do you know about that room being locked?"

"Your mother told me, but she didn't explain why."

"I can understand. No one is proud of having insanity in the family."

"People aren't ashamed of those things now."

"You don't know my folks, or you wouldn't say that," he argued. "They didn't let anyone near her."

"I think that was wrong."

"Don't condemn until you know," he argued. "I remember her well and she was strange. She wouldn't have been able to talk to anyone. She sat in silence most of the time."

"Poor thing!"

"*You* can say that," Johnny said. "Only at nights did I ever hear her. Then she'd walk the floor of her room and scream. You could hear those eerie screams up in my room!"

"The nights must have been a torment for her."

"Maybe," he said. "When I was a child, my parents warned me not to go near her when she sat on the patio. And I never did. She always wore black and she'd sit under an umbrella out there and not move for hours."

"When did she die?"

Johnny hesitated. Then he said, "I guess it must have been two or three years ago. I don't know. I haven't been here every summer."

She thought it a less than satisfactory answer. She had the feeling he wasn't telling her all the truth, that he was again being evasive—but she was used to that in him. But now she could understand about the locked room.

She said, "So your parents have kept that room locked ever since?"

"Yes. They had always reserved it for her. It was especially furnished so there was nothing there she could hurt herself with. I guess after she died they decided not to change anything, so they just shut it up."

"It's one of the best rooms in the house," she said.

"My father wanted it that way," Johnny said. "He would not stint his sister on anything even though she was mad. I think her insanity bothered him even more than it did my mother."

"And you never talked with this Aunt Grace?"

"No."

"What about Irma?"

"She used to visit her in her room with my mother, but she didn't stay or anything like that. And when Aunt Grace was out on the patio, Irma would sometimes bring her things like a soft drink or candy. I remember she liked candy."

"Poor demented soul!" Kim said. "Did she ever become violent again after that first time?"

"I can't say," Johnny replied impatiently. "I wish you would not go on talking about her. I don't find it the most pleasant of subjects."

"I'm sorry," she said.

"It's all right," he grumbled. "That gossipy old captain ought to have been able to find something else to talk to you about."

She said, "I think he was genuinely interested in whether your aunt was still alive. He felt I would know if she were here."

"Well, you told him she wasn't here, and that should settle it," Johnny said grimly.

When they arrived back at the old mansion, everything was quiet. There was no sign of Irma or Jim Blake when they went inside. Kim thanked Johnny for taking her for the drive and bade him good night. He indicated he was going to the billiards room for a while before going to bed.

Kim went on up the broad stairway, which was now in shadow. Not a sound disturbed the midnight quiet of the old mansion. She could hear the smallest squeaking of the floorboards as she made her way alone the hall. And when she came by the door of the room next to hers in which the mad Grace had spent her summers, she could not restrain a tiny shudder.

It had been a kind of macabre story that the ancient captain had told her. The thought of the quiet madwoman returning to the beloved scene of her childhood for the summer months, year after year, was a touching one. Kim wondered how she must have felt to obtain this annual freedom and what it must have been like to return to the mental hospital at the end of each summer.

From what Johnny had said, it was unlikely that the unfortunate madwoman knew much that was going on around her. So perhaps she had not minded. But one couldn't help worrying that she might have had moments of lucidity in which she knew the awful truth. Because she had tried to murder, she had been locked up for most of her life. What a dreadful thing to live with!

And the ancient captain had not let it go at that. He had strongly suggested that mental illness had appeared in various generations of the Craig family down through the years. No wonder that Stephen Craig had been terribly upset by his sister's madness and had warned his children not to go near her. The strain which had cursed his family must have been well known to him, and he would not want his own children to be tainted by any contact with it.

Strangely, from what Johnny had said, the family had not been as firm about Irma's avoiding the madwoman as they had about his conduct in this regard. Could it have been that even at an early age his parents had seen an erratic streak in him? Had they worried that contact with the madwoman might have a further unsettling effect on him? This thought raised itself up to send a surge of fear through her.

She prepared for bed quickly and turned out the lights. Before she settled into bed she opened one of the windows a bit so that she could hear the ocean. There was something definitely relaxing about the sound and the smell of the salt water that also pleased her.

In bed she stared up into the shadows and thought about all that had gone on in the short time since she'd arrived at Craig House. She had landed in the middle of a most puzzling situation, and it was made more confusing since she had not been able to make her mind up about Johnny.

He claimed that he had brought her to the house near Dark Harbor to try to discover whether Sheila Moore was a murderess. But was that his true reason? Or did he simply want to make the vivacious and lovely Sheila madly jealous, as he had down with the drowned Helen Walsh?

And what about the ghost? There were so many questions. She closed her eyes at this point and fell asleep. It was a sleep without dreams and it went on until she suddenly heard what seemed in her half-awake state to be a scream. The eerie sound in the middle of the night made her sit up in bed in alarm.

She stared into the darkness of her room and tried to decide whether the scream had been a part of a dream or whether she had really heard something!

And then—to answer her tortured nerves—the shape of a woman in a shimmering, tight-fitting evening gown gradually took form in the darkness! Kim gave a terrified gasp as the ghost of Helen Walsh came slowly toward her!

CHAPTER SEVEN

The apparition bore down on Kim. She shrieked and drew back against the pillows as far as she could but she was unable to escape the cold, dripping-wet hands of the ghost! She saw the seaweed-matted features of the phantom looming above her and then felt the cruel pressure of the icy, wet hands around her throat!

Unable to cry out or escape, she struggled briefly to free herself from the ghost and then sank into unconsciousness! When she finally opened her eyes and stirred on the bed with a moan, the room was still in darkness and the phantom appeared to have vanished. She groped for the light on her bedside table and at last found it and turned it on.

The room was empty! She touched a hand to her throat and tried to tell herself it had all been a nightmare. The stories she'd heard had preyed on her mind and caused her to dream of Helen Walsh returning in ghostly form. It had to be that!

She paced back and forth in the shadowed room, wanting to rouse someone and tell them her story and yet afraid to. She was almost sure she would be derided and her story dismissed as a bad dream. She went to the window and glanced out, but could see nothing. The roar of the waves came to her clearly and far out across the water the beam of Gull Light flashed across the dark sky.

Leaving the window, she was about to cross to her bed, but she thought she heard a sound—a sound like shuffling footsteps! And the sound came from the adjoining room! The locked room! With fear draining the color from her face, she turned to stare at the door linking her room to that other one. And at once she asked herself whether it might be unlocked. Had her eerie visitor come to her through that door?

She was trembling, and it required all her courage to slowly approach the door and try the knob. It was locked as it had always been. Not satisfied, she placed her ear close to the door jamb and listened. She scarcely breathed in her attempt to hear if there might be someone in that other room. The seconds went by. There was nothing but silence.

Frustrated, she moved away from the door and back to her bed. But there still lurked in her mind a question as to whether she had heard someone slowly moving about in there. She began to worry that Johnny and his family might have lied to her. Suppose mad old Grace might still be coming to the house as a summer visitor. Then it might have been the madwoman who had made the terrifying attack on her!

She lay in bed tormented by all these possibilities. She saw by the clock that it was two-thirty and dawn was still some time away. She could not bring herself to remain in the room and attempt to sleep unless she left the bedside lamp on. It gave her a little assurance.

At last her eyes closed and she slept until morning. When she awoke to another sunny, fine day, the lamp on her bedside table was still burning. Feeling somewhat guilty, she turned it off and got up.

There was no one in the dining room when she sat down there. The maid came and served her and she ate her entire breakfast without anyone else appearing. When she completed her morning meal, she went out to the patio and discovered Irma in her bathing suit. Johnny's sister was sunning herself on one of the lounges.

Irma waved to her and called out, "Why don't you change and join me? I'm going in a little later."

Kim strolled over to the poolside. "I may, after a while. I'd like to see Johnny. Has he been around?"

"He was up early," Irma said, her voluptuous figure enhanced by the daring red string bikini she had donned. "He may be in the study with my father discussing estate business."

"Perhaps," she said. "It's a lovely day." She sat on one of the colorful canvas chairs.

Irma raised herself up on an elbow and stared at her from the comfort of the lounge. "You look terribly pale! Aren't you feeling well?"

Her cheeks warming, Kim said, "I had a bad dream last night. I didn't sleep well."

"I should have thought the sea air here would make you sleep soundly," Johnny's sister said.

"I know," Kim agreed. "I had a busy day yesterday. I may have overdone it."

"Probably," Irma said. "I dream worst when I'm overtired."

"Most people do," Kim said. She found it difficult to talk with Johnny's assured sister.

"Of course, anyone who caters to Johnny is bound to be nervous," Irma went on. She got up from the lounge and went over to the pool to take out the thermometer hanging in the water on a string and check the temperature.

"Nearly eighty! I like the water warm."

"Is it a seawater pool?" Kim asked.

"Yes, we pipe it up from the shore. You must come in!"

"I will," she said. "As soon as I see Johnny, I'll go up to my room and change into my bathing suit."

Stretching out lazily on her stomach on the lounge again,

Irma asked, "Are you comfortable in your room?"

"Yes. It has a lovely view."

"I know," the other girl said. "It and the room next to it have the best views on that floor."

Trying hard to sound casual, Kim said, "You mean the room your Aunt Grace used to occupy."

Irma gave her a surprised look. "You've heard about her?"

"Yes."

"Weird story," Irma said. "She really went crazy. Tried to kill her sister. That was ages ago. They're both dead now."

"I see," she said carefully. "But this Grace did come here for the summer every year, didn't she?"

"Yes," Irma said. "Father and Mother fitted that room up like a padded cell. Aunt Grace never did come back to anything like sanity, so the room had to be bare of anything which might create a hazard. They left the room as it was. It's kept locked just as it was when she was in there, mad."

"Were you frightened of her?"

"A little," Irma admitted. "She used to come down here and sit on the patio. I was her favorite, but she didn't like Johnny."

"Oh?" This was new information.

"She didn't like Johnny at all," Irma said with satisfaction and a strange little smile on her tanned face. "And she hated one of the maids. You know what happened the last year she was here?"

"No."

Irma sat up and with a confidential air leaned forward and told her, "The maid came out here to bring her iced tea. She drank gallons of iced tea! And Aunt Grace suddenly came to life with a mad scream and began throttling her. I was in the pool. I thought I'd die! It was awful! The gardener came and rescued the maid and Mother took Aunt Grace up to her room, with Aunt Grace still screaming every step of the way. It created a stir here!"

"I can well imagine," Kim said.

"The maid had to be attended by a doctor, and there was talk of her taking it to court. But my mother and father paid her off and managed to keep the other servants from talking about it in Dark Harbor. You have no idea how my parents hate scandal."

"I know they are conservative people."

"So you can realize how popular mad Aunt Grace was with them. They had a discussion and agreed she was never to come here again. I think if they'd brought her here after that, the servants might have left."

"They didn't bring her back the next year?"

"No. And she died in hospital that summer. I don't know the details. My parents are very hush-hush about it all. They feel Aunt Grace was a shameful mark on the family name. I don't agree, but that doesn't much matter."

"It's a bizarre story," she said.

"Yes," Irma agreed. "We were afraid the Moores would get hold of it and spread it. Sheila is a gossip, as you well know, and that drunken father of hers is just as bad. But we kept it from them."

"That couldn't have been easy. Did Sheila come over here then as she does now?"

"She always has," Irma said with disgust. "But she and her father happened to be away on the Cape the week Aunt Grace went bonkers. So that helped."

"That was lucky."

Irma studied her from behind her dark sunglasses and said, "I hear you and Sheila went driving together yesterday."

Kim smiled ruefully. "I wasn't given much choice."

"Sheila would see to that. You want to watch her."

"I intend to."

"She probably wanted to get you alone and ask you a lot of questions about Johnny," Irma said. "Don't ever trust anything she tells you."

"I was on my guard."

"She wants Johnny for herself," Irma went on. "And the fact that you're here and Johnny and you are engaged won't stop her trying to get him. She's so used to having her own way in all things, she can't accept that Johnny doesn't want her for a wife."

"She made that fairly clear," Kim said. "But luckily I have had plenty of warning about her."

"She doesn't like me," Irma went on. "And she hates Jim Blake because he won a case against her father—some tax thing. She can't say anything bad enough about him."

"And she didn't get on with Helen Walsh either," Kim said.

Irma shook her head. "How she hated that poor girl! She had an idea Johnny was serious about her. I could have told her he wasn't, but you can't reason with Sheila."

"So I've heard," Kim said, rising from the canvas chair. "I'll see if I can find Johnny. I'll probably be back soon."

"I hope you do come," Irma said. "I'm about the only one who uses the pool, and it's lonely. Of course, Sheila wanders over when she gets tired of her own pool, but she's more of a nuisance than company!" Johnny's sister made a wry face and then went to the side of the pool and began lowering herself down the ladder into the sparkling blue water.

Kim turned and walked back toward the side entrance of the old mansion. She was close to the french doors which opened out there when she met Johnny. He was on his way out in shorts and an open-necked shirt.

"Hi!" he said. "I wondered where you were."

"I've been looking for you," she said.

"I was in the study with Dad," he told her. "And I made a couple of long-distance calls. I have a chance to star at Falmouth next month if I want to. Maybe I can get you in the company as well."

"I'd like that," she said.

"I'll know later," Johnny told her. "They want me to do *The Prisoner of Second Avenue*. I'd like to do it if I can get the terms I asked."

She smiled ruefully. "Is the money so important?"

"I have my price," the handsome young star said. "Why were you looking for me?"

Kim glanced around to make sure they were alone and not liable to be overheard. Then, with a serious look on her pretty face, she said, "I have something to tell you. Something happened last night."

"What?"

"I had a visitor. The ghost of Helen Walsh!"

His mouth gaped open. "You're not starting that!"

"Honestly!" she said.

"Tell me about it," he said, almost harshly.

"I awoke from a deep sleep and this thing was in the room. A phantom, dripping wet and covered with seaweed, almost exactly as Sheila described it."

"She upset you with her stories!"

"No! The phantom came and tried to throttle me with her cold wet hands and I blacked out. When I came to, she had gone. But I know she was there!"

"You had a nightmare!" Johnny protested. "Not that I blame you. It's what comes of being with Sheila yesterday."

"You're wrong!" she protested. "This had nothing to do with Sheila. I heard a noise in the adjoining room."

"That room is empty!"

"I heard shuffling footsteps in there," she insisted weakly.

Johnny's handsome face was shadowed with annoyance. "How can you say that?"

"Because it's true. I'm certain of it."

"The room is kept locked," he asserted. "No one ever goes in there."

"I can't help it!" She knew it was a lost cause. She'd known it before she began the argument. But she had to try! She needed to try and make him understand.

He took her by the arms and spoke earnestly to her. "Kim, I don't blame you for these flights of fancy. You've been under a heavy strain. But don't give way to these ideas. I need your help in setting a trap for Sheila. You won't be any use to me if you begin to outrival her in neurotic fancies."

Kim shook her head gloomily. "I knew you wouldn't listen to me."

"Then why did you come to me with this story?"

"I hoped I might be wrong—that you'd understand!"

"I *do* understand," he said. "And I will help. We can begin by making no more mention of this. As far as I'm concerned, I never heard this ghost business."

"What will that solve?"

"If we don't talk about it, you won't be dwelling on it," he said. "I'm on my way down to Mack Carter's boat-building place. Come along with me."

She hesitated. "I told Irma I'd join her at the pool."

"You can when you come back," he said. "It's only a short way, and I won't be there long."

With a sigh, she said, "All right. And you're not going to pay any attention at all to what I told you?"

He smiled wearily. "I'll make one concession. When I come back, I'll find out for sure whether that room has been used lately. I know it hasn't. But I'll get a key and take a look myself. Does that make you feel better?"

"Not much," she said. "But at least it will be a start."

"Come on," he said, his arm around her. "We'll use the station wagon this morning."

He drove the big wagon out onto the main highway and then took the road in the opposite direction to Dark Harbor.

She said, "This is the road which leads to the monastery, isn't it?"

"Yes," he agreed, "but we aren't going that far."

They drove about a quarter mile and then he turned off on one of the many side roads which ran from the highway to the shore. They passed a painted sign which announced they were on the property of Carter Shipbuilders and drove on until they came to a wide cove with a dock and a number of battered buildings on it.

"We've arrived," he said, bringing the big wagon to a halt.

They got out and walked down to the first building which had a crude sign lettered "Office" on it. There she saw Mack Carter in working clothes in conversation with a smartly dressed Derek Mills. The two men were standing on the platform outside the building, and she recognized the museum director at once.

She and Johnny joined the other two and there were greetings all around. It seemed that Derek Mills was there in connection with repairs on a boat used by the museum. Johnny at once began an argument with the lazy but amiable Mack Carter concerning the delay in finishing Irma's boat.

Derek Mills turned to her and began a conversation. "I hope you haven't forgotten my invitation to inspect the museum," he said.

"I haven't," she told him. "It's been a matter of time. But I should manage it within a few days."

The good-looking brown-haired man gave her a questioning look as he asked, "How are you enjoying Dark Harbor?"

"I find it most interesting," she said.

"It has a long history," he told her. "You can learn a lot of it in a short time at the museum."

Johnny finished his business with Mack Carter and in none too good a mood turned to Kim and said he was ready to leave. She bade Derek Mills a hasty good-bye and they walked back up to the station wagon. Johnny helped her in and closed her door. Then he went around to sit behind the wheel. In the meanwhile, Mack Carter had evidently remembered something he wished to discuss with Johnny.

The big man came lumbering up the hill, leaving Derek Mills alone on the platform in front of the office. Johnny sat at the wheel with the car door open on his side and a dark look on his handsome face.

"This fellow is a near dolt!" he murmured to her as Mack Carter approached the car with a genial grin on his broad, weathered face.

Mack Carter was puffing as he came up to the station wagon. "Sorry, Mr. Craig," he said, "but I didn't ask whether you wanted us to paint a name on the dory when we finish it."

"Of course!" Johnny said impatiently. "Same as before. Put Irma's name on it."

"I will, Mr. Craig," the stout man said, beaming. "I'll see she has the name *Irma C.* on her!" He was standing holding the pillar by the front window of the car as he talked.

Kim was vaguely conscious of this and it disturbed her, but she didn't like to speak out about it. Then, to her utter horror, she saw Johnny slowly bringing the door to as he went on talking and holding the stout man's attention. It was like someone slowly going about springing a trap. And then very suddenly Johnny brought the door shut and she could hear the crunch on the unfortunate Mack Carter's fingers.

She screamed, but too late for it to be a warning. Mack Carter stood there with a look of shock and then horror on his broad face. Johnny cried out an oath and swung the door open again.

"Did I get you?" he asked the stout man.

Mack Carter had gone pale and he was holding his crushed, bloodied fingers up as if he couldn't believe what had just happened. In a faint voice, he said, "You jammed me!"

From his vantage point on the platform Derek Mills had seen the entire thing. He came running up beside the big man and with a single glance at the injured hand, said, "That's nasty! I'll take you in to Dr. Taylor."

"I can take him," Johnny said, stepping out of the wagon.

"No," Derek Mills said, almost sternly. "Let me do it." And he led a shaken Mack Carter away. The big man stumbled along as if he might faint at any moment.

Johnny stood there watching until the other two were in Derek Mills's car and it was racing up the rough, hilly road on its way to the doctor's office. Then he got behind the wheel of the station wagon and closed the door. He was red-faced and clearly upset.

As he started the station wagon, he glanced at Kim in a guilty fashion and said, "That old fool caused that accident by his own carelessness."

Shocked, she replied in a low voice, "He was careless, but you must have seen his hand."

"I wasn't watching his hand!" Johnny exclaimed angrily, starting to turn in a frenzied fashion and making the tires squeal.

"I saw you close the door on his fingers!"

"Don't keep harping on it!" Johnny exclaimed in a rage as he crouched over the wheel and drove up the hill much too fast.

"You were as much to blame as he was!"

"He's an old clown!"

"I feel sorry for him," she said stoutly.

He gave her an angry glance. "Well, now you have something else to hold against me!"

"You talk as if I want to hold things against you," she said.

"Don't you?"

"You know I don't, but I've seen you be careless so many times. You know your reputation! I can't forget that you caused Babs Darriot to have that awful fall that put her out of the show!"

"I paid her the salary she lost, didn't I?" he said.

"That doesn't change things."

He uttered another oath under his breath. They reached the main highway, and he drove with a little more care. She imagined that Derek Mills would have the injured man at the doctor's by this time. And she wondered what the museum director must have thought about the accident. He also had seen it all. She felt a good deal of relief as he drove her into the estate parking lot.

He turned to her as he shut off the engine. "Anyway I brought you back safely."

"Thanks," she said crisply, and got out of the car and went up to her room. At that moment she wanted no more talk with him. She changed to her bathing suit and then went down to the pool. When she reached it, she found that Sheila had come over to join Irma. Both girls were swimming as she reached the poolside.

Irma stood up in the shallow end of the pool to say, "Where were you?"

She said, "I went down with Johnny to see about your boat."

Irma was very interested. "What's the good word?"

"I think it will soon be ready. That is, if Mr. Carter is able to work on it. He had an accident while we were there."

"An accident?" Sheila rose out of the water and came to the side of the pool where Kim was standing. "What sort of accident?"

She hesitated. "It wasn't anything major, but it was nasty enough. Mack Carter caught his hand in the station wagon door."

"Oh, no!" Irma protested.

An odd smile crossed Sheila's oval face. She asked Kim, "You mean that Johnny closed the door on Mack's hand, don't you?"

"Something like that," she reluctantly admitted.

Sheila continued to smile up at her. "And you're so upset! You oughtn't to be! I told you what he's like—some of the things he's done."

"It was an accident," Kim protested.

"Of course it was," Sheila laughed. "An accident created by Johnny!" And she swung around in the water and swam in the direction of the deep end of the pool.

Irma gazed after her with distaste and then told Kim, "You mustn't listen to her! Get into the pool and enjoy yourself!"

She did, but the unpleasant incident remained in her mind to trouble her. Sheila left the pool first and walked back toward her own place. She had refrained from taunting Kim anymore about the accident, but she'd already said enough to make her worry more.

After lunch Kim was restless. She asked Irma if she might borrow her small red sports car and was given immediate permission to use it. She drove away from the imposing old mansion with the feeling that she was escaping from a prison. It had been a bad morning, and she wanted to see Derek Mills and find out how the accident victim had fared.

She knew the general direction to the museum, and arrived there after making only one wrong turn. The modern concrete building was situated on a hill, and though it had none of the island's quaintness in its exterior, it was a treasure place inside. She inquired at the reception desk and was told she would find Derek Mills upstairs in his office.

She made her way through the downstairs gallery with its many marine paintings on the walls and the various exhibitions of model ship carving set out on stands at a number of spots in the big room. Passing all this by, she ascended the stairs and went straight to the sign which said "Director." The door was open and she saw Derek Mills at his desk.

Knocking lightly on the door frame, she said, "May I come in?"

Derek Mills glanced up and at once looked pleased to see her. He rose and came around to greet her, "My dear Miss Rice, so you have finally kept your word."

"I decided I'd waited long enough," she said.

"Good," he told her. "Do sit down. Would you like some coffee? I have it iced at this time of year."

"I'd enjoy a glass," she said.

"Fine," he said. He went outside to the adjoining office and ordered the coffee for them. Then he returned and took his seat behind the desk.

Awkwardly she asked him, "What about that poor man's hand?"

His expression became serious. "That was an ugly business."

"How badly was he hurt?"

"I took him straight to the doctor's," Derek Mills said, "and happily Dr. Taylor was in. The hand is a mess. It was a question whether two of the fingers might have to be amputated."

"How awful!"

"I agree," Derek Mills said soberly. "I'm glad to say that Dr. Taylor thinks he may save all the fingers. At least he has done repairs. Now we'll have to wait and see how the hand turns out after a few days."

"I feel so sorry for Mr. Carter," she said.

"He's suffering a good deal of pain," Derek Mills agreed. "And there is the worry that he may eventually have to lose those fingers."

"It was a dreadful moment," Kim recalled.

A bright young woman came in with the two glasses of iced coffee on a tray. When she had served them, she went out and closed the office door after her.

Derek Mills held up his glass. "To a pleasant meeting," he said.

She took her glass and said, "Thank you. I've looked forward to coming here. I didn't expect such an ugly event would hurry me in my visit."

"I know it must have been bad for you," the young museum director sympathized. "But I was so concerned for Carter that I didn't say anything to you. I could think only of getting him in the car before he fainted and heading for the doctor's."

"I understood that," she said. And then, after a difficult moment of hesitation, she went on. "I hardly know how to tell you this. But you were there. You must have seen it happen."

"I did," he said.

She gave him a frightened look. "I hate to say it, but I think that Johnny did it deliberately."

"I know," Derek Mills said solemnly.

She was relieved. "You think so too?"

He nodded slowly. "As you say, I saw it happen. And from where I stood, it seemed he drew that door closed slyly and without offering poor Mack Carter any warning."

"You're right," she said.

"It would do no good to argue the point," Derek warned her. "He'd be bound to deny it."

"I know," she said miserably. "I took him to task, and he only became enraged."

"That's in character."

She gave Derek a troubled look. "What does it mean?"

"It means that Johnny Craig hasn't changed."

"Then you know about him?"

"I have to," the museum director said grimly. "I grew up here and knew him as a boy. I was a little older, but I still heard enough and saw enough to make me wonder about him."

"He has a terribly cruel streak!"

"That has been duly reported in the scandal sheets," Derek Mills said. "And for once, I don't think they exaggerated too much."

Kim said, "You mean those girls who were in accidents when in his company?"

"If you'd call them accidents."

She said, "I met him in Boston. We worked in a play together. Several things happened which worried me." And she proceeded to tell him about them.

Derek Mills listened gravely. Then he said, "In view of what you've said and all your suspicions, I wonder that you are here in the role of his bride-to-be, Miss Rice."

She sat back in her chair and suddenly decided that she must explain her position to someone. It seemed all-important to her that someone should know the truth.

She said, "My being his bride-to-be is strictly a role, and nothing more than that."

He showed puzzlement. "I'm not sure I understand."

"Johnny hired me to come down here. He told me he wanted me as protection against Sheila Moore. He said she was trying to force him to marry her."

"Sheila has always been in love with him. And when it comes to deviousness, she is his match," Derek Mills agreed.

"I came here with the guarantee that all I had to do was be pleasant and remain on the scene. Then after I arrived here I heard about the mysterious drowning of Helen Walsh. Johnny admitted that he suspected Sheila of pushing her over the side. He also said he had brought me on the scene as a decoy to try and trap Sheila into some sort of attack on me and thus give herself away on Helen's drowning."

"Some weird story!" Derek Mills exclaimed.

"There is more to it than that," she told him.

"Please continue," he said.

"Sheila claims she sees Helen Walsh's ghost regularly. She delights in telling this when Johnny is around, and it enrages him."

"I can imagine."

"He claims she is making the whole thing up. But he still believes that she took advantage of a drunken Helen and shoved her off that pleasure boat because she feared that he might be going to marry her."

Derek Mills looked grim. "Knowing Sheila, I can only say that it is only all too possible."

"And now *I'm* to be the target," Kim said.

"I think Johnny is wrong in exposing you to such danger," the museum director said. "And I think you made a mistake in coming here under false pretenses."

"I realize that now," she admitted.

"Johnny will have no qualms about risking your life," Derek Mills continued. "He treated poor Helen Walsh badly, and I'd say helped contribute to her death. He took her to that drunken party and left her alone."

"He always has an excuse for whatever happens," she said. "I find it a strange house. The family worships Johnny and thinks he can do no wrong. Yet they all seem continually frightened."

"Perhaps they know what a risk he is," Derek Mills suggested.

"Last night I had an intruder in my room," she said, and she proceeded to tell him about it. She finished with, "They all are acting so strangely about that room I wonder if that mad old Grace mightn't still be hidden in there and that it was she who tried to throttle me."

"I'd find that an easier explanation than Helen Walsh's ghost," Derek admitted.

"I never met Helen Walsh," Kim said, "but I've come to feel a great sympathy for her in death. I've stayed on here only because I'd like to bring about the capture of her murderer, if she was murdered. And Johnny seems positive Sheila is the guilty one."

Derek Mills gave her a knowing look. "That could be because Johnny doesn't have all the facts."

CHAPTER EIGHT

Kim stared at the good-looking museum director in wonder. "You mean there are some things about the tragedy which Johnny doesn't know?"

"It could well be."

"I'm not sure I follow you."

"Certain information came my way which indicated someone else might have had a motive to murder Helen Walsh," Derek Mills said. "You know she loved a good time and dated a number of young men."

"I heard she was a kind of party girl," Kim agreed.

"I don't want to repeat what I was told," Derek said, "but I do want to help you."

"Believe me, I'm in need of help," Kim told him.

Derek asked, "Have you met Dr. Taylor?"

"Yes. Twice, in fact. Once at a cocktail party at Sheila's and then again in Dark Harbor."

"I suggest that you go down and talk to him," the museum director told her. "Give him all the information you've given me and ask him what he thinks might have happened to Helen Walsh. I have an idea you'll be interested in what he tells you."

Kim deduced by the seriousness of the young man's tone that the facts the doctor might offer her would have an important bearing on the tragedy.

She said, "Do you think the doctor will want to confide in me?"

"I'm sure he will," Derek said. "Don't call on him until tonight, after his office hours. Drop by at about eight o'clock. He ought to be free by then, and I'll phone him in the meantime."

"You're being very kind to me," she said. "I was afraid you might think me a highly unreliable and neurotic female."

"Not at all," he said. "Since I know Johnny Craig so well, I can be sympathetic."

"There are times when I cannot help but like him," she said worriedly. "He has a lot of talent and he could be somebody very special. But there is that strange strain in him."

"I understand," Derek Mills said with a slight frown. "I blame it on heredity. There has been madness in the Craig family down through the years. I think Johnny has been touched by it, yet not enough for anyone to call him truly insane."

"Even though some of his actions border on the insane," she said. "Crushing that poor man's hand as he did today is an example."

"A sickening business," he agreed.

"There are two sides to him."

"You know, I'm afraid he's heading for worse trouble, especially after what I saw this morning."

"I'm frightened. Especially about the figure which came into my room."

"I can't offer you any help there," he said. "Though I do recall that up until a few years ago Grace Craig was always brought here for the summer. My mother knew her and used to pay her an annual visit."

"What did your mother report about her?"

"She said it was very sad. Grace Craig had lost a lot of weight, and looked much older than she should, and she just sat in her chair and stared without saying anything. Mother felt there was no recognition at all. The last couple of years my mother gave up. She felt she was only embarrassing the family by calling and she was certain Grace Craig was too mad to know her."

"That fits what I've already heard," she said. "They don't like to talk about her."

Derek sighed. "I think it is the fear of hereditary madness which truly bothers them. And I have an idea they are especially worried about Johnny."

"Sheila Moore says such awful things about him," Kim said. "And yet it seems she wants to marry him."

Derek Mills smiled sadly. "It is difficult to explain people in love. They rarely show any response to reason. It is possible that Sheila recognizes Johnny as a troubled person, and yet cannot help herself being in love with him."

"It has to be something like that," she agreed. "He has an offer to star in a play in Falmouth. He is considering it now, and he wants to try to get me a role in the play if he accepts."

"If he does take the engagement, it might be a good thing," Derek said. "It would get you away from Pirate Island, and I doubt you'd decide to come back."

"I probably wouldn't return," she said. "While I'm here I seem to be under a kind of spell. It seems urgent that the mystery surrounding the death of Helen Walsh should be explained. But once I leave here, I'm certain it wouldn't be all that important to me."

"You're probably right."

She gave the museum director a searching look. "I wonder that the police weren't more concerned about that girl's drowning. You would think they'd be suspicious."

Derek Mills sat back in his swivel chair. "I don't think they were satisfied, but they couldn't push the investigation any further. No one could be found who saw her fall overboard.

Without witnesses, it had to remain a mystery. But there was plenty of gossip."

"I can imagine."

"A drunken private party with a noted screen star aboard," Derek said grimly. "Rumors were bound to fly. Especially since Helen was Johnny's date that night. But after a period of time, the gossip died down. Now it's almost forgotten."

"Not by certain people," she said.

"I know that," Derek agreed. "I can only repeat: go and see Dr. Taylor. If you want to call on me for help of any kind, I'm at your service. I think you've managed to get yourself in a bad spot, and I'd like to see you get off the island."

"Thank you," she said, rising. "I will come back and see you since you're so kind."

Derek Mills rose from his desk to accompany her out. "Part of my duties here include taking care of the problems of visitors. I think you have a problem serious enough to warrant my attention."

"Thank you," she said sincerely.

His serious brown eyes met hers. "Now remember—get in touch with me if things suddenly take a turn for the worse."

"I will," she promised and thanked him again as she left.

She went down the stairs to the main lobby of the museum, impressed by the charm of the young director and mystified about the information Dr. Henry Taylor might give her.

She was now in the gallery of paintings on her way out when she suddenly found herself face-to-face with the ancient Captain Miller. The old man had a straight-stemmed pipe in his mouth which he took out as he gave her a smile of greeting and removed his peaked cap.

"So you came up to see the displays," the old captain said

with a friendly twinkle in the surprisingly youthful blue eyes set in his lined face.

"Yes," she said. "And I had a chat with Derek Mills."

"Fine young man," Captain Miller said. "I've just finished my lecture in the annex room. Had all of two dozen visitors to hear me!"

"That seems a reasonable group for a fine afternoon," she said.

He nodded. "Yep. No complaints on that score. Trouble is, I get too many retired female schoolteachers. I'd like to get a younger audience."

She smiled. "I'm sure you would if they knew what you were like."

"Thank you," the old man said. "Seen all the paintings? There are a half-dozen Augustus Johns, a couple of Wyeths and some other paintings by people without big reputations but with plenty of talent."

She turned to glance at the large painting of a very plain house with a kind of inverted horseshoe on its chimney. She said, "That's interesting because the house is so plain."

Captain Zachary turned to it with interest. "Has a history, that one!"

"Really?"

"Yep," the old man said, staring at it. "The Historical Society here commissioned a fellow to paint it about thirty-odd years ago. Artist who did it was an Englishman named Watts who was invalided in the Second World War. He was married to a local girl and came here to try to recover. He did some good paintings, but he didn't recover. He's buried here in the local cemetery."

"That is sad," she said. "The painting has a brownish sort of melancholy tone, and the house looks lonely standing by itself."

"The oldest house on the island," the captain said. "The Jethro Adams House. It's called the Horseshoe House too."

"Because of the decoration on the chimney?" she suggested.

"That's right," he said. "The house was built in 1686. It was a wedding present to Jethro and his bride. Some people say the decoration is a tuning fork or a wishbone, but most people settle for it being a horseshoe."

"Thanks for telling me about it," she said.

"About all I'm useful for these days—giving out a lot of dead information. How is Johnny Craig?"

"He keeps busy," she said, not wanting to mention the incident at the boat yard.

"Did you ask him about his Aunt Grace?"

"Yes. He says she is dead."

"Well, that could be, though I never heard of it. I wonder there wasn't at least a listing of her death in the Dark Harbor weekly. They keep a line on all the people who live here—even the summer people."

"Perhaps you missed the item," she suggested.

"That could be," Captain Zachary agreed. "You have your car with you?"

"Yes," she said. "Can I give you a lift?"

He looked pleased. "If you wouldn't mind. My old car is in the garage. It's kind of an antique like myself, but I miss it."

They left the museum together and following his directions she drove him to a picture-book cottage on a side street off the Main Street. He told her that his wife had died a few years earlier, but he was loath to give up his house.

"She's a trim little craft," he said, standing in his driveway and admiring the cottage, "and the last one in which I'm liable to be captain. So I just want to remain with it."

"I think you're wise," she said.

"You and Johnny come and see me some evening," the old man invited her.

"Thank you," she said. "I'll speak to him about it."

She drove on back to Craig House, filled with the talk of the afternoon. Her main problem now was going to be returning to the village. She badly wanted to see Dr. Taylor and talk to him, but she could well imagine some questions being asked if she said she wanted the use of Irma's car again.

She decided to get as near to the truth as possible. She would tell Johnny she wanted to consult the doctor. And she would give her difficulty in sleeping as an excuse, say she wanted to get some sleeping pills. Having arrived at that decision, she felt better. She hoped that the others at Craig House would accept this explanation. Then she'd have no trouble getting away for the eight o'clock appointment which Derek Mills had promised to arrange.

When she drove in, she saw Johnny standing on the patio in a striking white suit with a drink in his hand. He waved to her and called out for her to join him when she'd parked the car. She knew that she had best go along with this if she wanted to keep him in good humor and get back to Dark Harbor to see Dr. Taylor.

She walked over to the patio and he greeted her with a smile. He said, "I didn't know you were away driving. I've been looking for you everywhere."

She managed a return smile. "I decided I'd like to see the museum."

"So that's where you've been!" He seemed in good humor.

"Yes."

"Let me make you a martini. I've asked the others to come down for a drink before dinner, but there's no telling when they'll straggle down."

"Your suit is very smart," she said.

"I decided to dress up," he told her. "There's a dance at the yacht club later. I'd like to take you." He handed her the drink.

Taking the martini from him, she told him, "I can't go until later. I've made an appointment to see the doctor at eight."

He showed surprise. "Dr. Taylor?"

"Yes."

"Why?"

"I haven't been sleeping well. I've had bad headaches and dreams. I'd like to get his opinion and have him give me some sleeping pills."

Johnny's handsome face darkened. "This isn't because of what happened this morning? Were you that badly upset?"

"Nothing like that," she protested.

He looked at her with troubled eyes. "I want you to believe that was an accident. I couldn't avoid jamming his hand. I didn't mean to."

"I know," she said tautly. "Better not to go over it."

"You think I have some kind of a crazy, cruel streak," he said, ignoring her advice. "You've always thought it because of the things you've read in the papers. You accused me of causing that old woman's accident in Boston. And I imagine you think I scalded your hand on purpose!"

He was carried away by his tirade and stood there scowling and red-faced. She shook her head. "Johnny, you mustn't! I don't want you upsetting yourself like this. I thought we'd agreed to say no more about this morning. Let us keep to that!"

He sighed. "All right," he said reluctantly.

"My visiting the doctor has to do with my own problem and nothing else."

TERROR AT DARK HARBOR

Johnny said, "I can drive you there and then we can go on to the yacht club."

"No."

His eyes widened. "Why not?"

Wearily, she said, "You'll make me nervous being there. Let me drive there myself and then come back here and dress for the dance. I don't want to make a visit to the doctor in an evening gown. I'd feel foolish."

He listened to her and said, "I suppose that makes sense. We don't have to get to the dance until ten. That ought to give you plenty of time."

"It will," she said, sipping her drink.

She was seated on one of the patio chairs and he was standing by her. He said, "What did Derek Mills have to say?"

"He was charming."

"I'll bet," Johnny said dryly. "You better watch out. You know, he's the most eligible man on the island right now. Since his wife died, a half-dozen girls have tried to interest him."

"And he's not shown any interest in marrying again?"

"No."

"He's very reserved. There is sort of a sadness about him," Kim observed.

Johnny gave her a twisted smile. "That's his way of getting female attention. He plays the role to perfection. I can see that he already has you converted to him."

She blushed. "Not at all."

"He'll be at the yacht club dance tonight, if that is any enticement for you."

She said, "Will Sheila be going?"

"I expect so," he said. "She always does."

"I wondered."

Johnny gave her a knowing look. "You'll have another chance to be at the same party. It will be interesting to see how she behaves toward you tonight."

"I don't enjoy that prospect particularly," she said.

"Don't forget it's one of the main reasons you're here," Johnny told her. "I want to discover how far Sheila's jealousy will take her."

"If what you've told me is true, it took her to the point of murder last time," she said. "Is that what you want again?"

Johnny's expression was grim. "I don't mean to allow anything like that to happen this time. But I *do* want to discover whether she really did murder Helen Walsh or not."

She said, "Helen had a number of other men friends besides you, didn't she?"

He looked annoyed. "Not all that many."

"But she did date others?"

"Yes."

"Anyone in particular besides yourself?" Kim asked.

"I wouldn't know," he said in a guarded voice. "I wasn't here on the island a whole lot. And she wouldn't tell me who she dated when she was here alone."

"Surely you'd hear from others?"

"I didn't make any inquiries," Johnny said stiffly. "I never did regard Helen as my exclusive property."

"I see," she said. "Who will be taking Sheila to the dance tonight?"

"Her father," he said. "That is, if he's sober enough. A good deal of the time he isn't."

Their conversation was interrupted at this point by Irma's joining them. Johnny's sister was dressed for the evening in a chic summer gown in an exotic print. Kim excused herself on the grounds of freshening up for dinner and went up to her room.

She was both pleased and worried. Pleased that she'd so easily managed to explain her planned visit to Dr. Taylor, and worried that Johnny had shown such a psychotic anger when he'd charged her with not being fair to him about the accident that morning. She had never seen him so near the edge of violence.

Once again at dinner, Kim was aware of the atmosphere of brooding fear which seemed to loom over the Craig family. Johnny tried to make some light conversation and was aided to a degree by Irma. But his parents continued to be gloomy, and the meal turned out to be another grim ordeal.

Kim was glad to have an excuse to get away from the old mansion as soon as dinner was over. She barely managed to get to Dr. Taylor's office by eight o'clock. As it turned out, there was no real hurry, since he still had several other patients to see. She buried herself in a magazine while the others were being taken care of. Not until the old doctor came to greet her did she rise from her chair.

"Derek told me you would be here," he said. "Come in." He ushered her into an office whose walls were lined with books. There was an examining table in a room which could be seen through a door at the rear and a large, framed medical certificate over the room's fireplace. The chairs were large and covered with leather. They had a well-worn look as if many patients had gone through the office in the years of the old man's practice.

She sat down opposite him and said, "It is kind of you to make time for me."

He brushed this aside with a wave of his hand. "Not at all," he said. "Derek told me why you wished to see me and filled me in on your position at Craig House. I must say I am rather alarmed."

"Things are not what they should be," she admitted.

"How did you let Johnny Craig talk you into such an arrangement?" Dr. Taylor wanted to know.

She sighed. "I can't honestly tell you. Maybe he has a kind of hypnotic power. I normally would never agree to do such a thing."

"I would think not," the white-haired doctor said. "Derek tells me you were visited by some phantom figure and attacked by it. But Johnny refused to give any credence to what happened."

"That is right," she said.

"There seems to be some question whether Grace is still brought to Craig House for the summer," the doctor said. "You say her room is kept carefully locked?"

"Yes."

"That suggests something," Dr. Taylor said. "No one I know has seen the old woman arrive—but that doesn't mean they haven't brought her here."

"They claim they haven't," Kim said. "But there is a strange tension in the house. It's a place of fear. They promised the summer help they wouldn't bring Grace Craig back again after she attacked the maid. And now they claim Grace is dead. But I wonder if they aren't secretly still bringing her here and don't want it known."

"If so, that would explain the attack on you," the friendly old doctor said.

She grimaced. "Otherwise I'll have to believe that I have seen the same ghost as Sheila—that the phantom figure of Helen Walsh attacked me."

The doctor looked solemn. "According to Derek, you were told by Johnny that Sheila toppled that unhappy girl off the pleasure boat."

"That is what he insists," she said. "And Sheila *does* act

strangely. She insists she continually sees the ghost of Helen."

"I find that all very odd," the veteran doctor said. "I know that Sheila is madly in love with Johnny. She always has been, despite his faults. But I can't see her murdering for him."

"Nor can I," Kim said.

"I think Sheila knows more than she is willing to admit," the doctor went on. "And I think Johnny has told you a pack of lies."

"It very well could be," she said. "Derek Mills suggested that you had information which might give a clue to who might be Helen's murderer."

"*If* she were murdered," the old man warned her. "She was very drunk at the time she went overboard. It could have been an accident."

"Somehow I don't feel it was."

"Neither do I," Dr. Taylor admitted. "The transactions between a doctor and his patient are sacred. You understand that?"

"Yes."

His shrewd eyes behind the horn-rimmed glasses met hers as he said, "Helen Walsh was my patient."

"Oh?"

He smiled ruefully. "That is not so odd. I'm the only doctor on the island. She had to come to me or go to the mainland."

"I'm sure she would have confidence in you," Kim said.

"She did. And what I'm about to tell you I would not divulge unless she were dead—and only because your own position is so desperate."

"Please go on," she said.

"Helen Walsh was a modern girl who partied a lot," the

old man said dryly. "She was a poor girl who gained entry into society here by being what I can only frankly designate as promiscuous."

"I gathered that from what I heard about her."

"Mind you, I'm not condemning her," the old man said. "She was pretty and kindhearted and she had a desire to enjoy some of the good things of life. Not too many are available to a clerk in a small store on this island. So she found her own way."

"I think Johnny was fond of her."

"I hope so," Dr. Taylor said. "Frankly, of all the men she knew, he was the one who most abused her. Just as I'm afraid he is apt to show cruelty to any woman close to him."

"That I know about," she said wryly.

The old doctor gave her a sober look. "Helen Walsh had one other man friend whom she saw almost as much as Johnny. You won't guess who it was. Few islanders know about it since they had secret meetings and their affair wasn't generally known. But you have met the man."

"I haven't met many people since I arrived on the island," she said.

"You *have* met Jim Blake."

"Jim Blake!" she gasped. "He and Irma are engaged."

"That's only a recent event," the old doctor said grimly. "Johnny and the rest of the Craig family were away from Dark Harbor all during the autumn, winter, and spring. It was during this time that Jim and Helen had their romance."

"That's almost impossible to believe," she said.

"Jim is very smooth. He is not one of the summer people, but a local lawyer who has managed to get in with the summer crowd. Once he manages a marriage with Irma, the Craig fortune will be in his future. And that is why he couldn't let Helen Walsh spoil it for him."

"I don't understand," she said.

"You will," the veteran doctor promised. "Some months ago Helen Walsh came to me and asked me to tell her if she were pregnant. I made the usual tests and told her that she was. It was then that she broke down in this office and sobbed that her romance with Johnny would be at an end. I asked her who the father of the child was, and she said 'Jim Blake.' She even traced the date of conception to a trip they made together to Boston in January."

"Then Helen was several months pregnant when she was drowned?" Kim said.

"Yes. And, if you'll remember, Jim Blake was aboard that boat. I wonder if Helen hadn't threatened him, demanded that he marry her, and in desperation he decided to bring about her death."

Kim was thoroughly shocked. "It's an entirely new line of thought on the tragedy," she said.

"I know," Dr. Taylor said. "I've debated whether I should go to the police or not. There's nothing I can prove against Jim Blake. I can say only that he had a strong motive for causing Helen's drowning. Whether he did it or not is another matter."

"I see him as a much more logical suspect than Sheila," Kim said.

"So do I. And so does Derek Mills," the doctor said. "That is why he felt I should let you in on this secret which I have so far withheld even from the police."

She opened her hands in a gesture of despair. "I don't know what to think now."

"No wonder," he said.

She said, "I was sure Irma and Jim Blake were free of all the dark happenings. Now it seems they are as badly off as Johnny or Sheila."

"Irma knows nothing about Jim and Helen," the old doctor said.

"I have never really liked Jim Blake," she said. "There is something false about him."

"A young man eager to get ahead," Dr. Taylor said. "I'm afraid he doesn't care what he has to do to manage it."

Kim said, "I feel more than ever that I should leave Craig House and Dark Harbor."

"It would be wise."

"Johnny plans to take me to the dance tonight. All the others will be there. I don't know that I can face it."

The old doctor's face wore a cynical look. "I'm afraid you made yourself a bargain and as long as you are here you will have to play your role as best you can. Your safety may depend on it."

"I'm afraid of those people and that house!"

"At least now you have Derek and me to confide in," the old doctor said. "No one will go too far unless they are certain they won't be suspected. That may insure your safety for a short while. If I were you, I'd go to the dance and try and enjoy myself."

"I'll try," she said unhappily. "I'm not at all sure how well I'll do." And she rose.

The old doctor was also on his feet. He said, "You'll manage. And remember, not a word to anyone about what I've told you. I may talk to the police within the next few days. When I do, I'll let you know."

Kim drove back to Craig House in a kind of dazed state. It had never occurred to her that Jim Blake might have been one of Helen Walsh's lovers. And now that she knew of the drowned girl's pregnancy by him, she could understand that he would have been desperate to protect his engagement to the wealthy Irma. Johnny did not know about all this, and that was why he suspected Sheila of the girl's murder.

It was after dark when she parked the car and went inside. She rushed upstairs and quickly changed into an evening gown, did some work with her hair, and touched up her makeup. She was back downstairs again by nine-forty and found Johnny waiting for her rather impatiently in the reception hall.

He told her, "Jim and Irma have gone ahead. We'd better get on our way or we'll be late."

"Fine," she said, relieved that the others had gone.

On the drive over to the yacht club, Johnny asked her, "What was the doctor's verdict?"

"Verdict?"

"About your headaches and sleeplessness," he said, glancing at her from the wheel.

"Oh," she said. "He thinks I'm overtired. He gave me some sleeping pills. I'm to go back again after a week or so. That is, if I'm still on the island."

"Why won't you be?"

"What about the play in Falmouth?" she said.

"I'd forgotten about it," he admitted. "I'll hear about it the first of the week."

"I'd like to do a play this summer," she said.

He gave her a one-sided smile. "You're already working. Aren't you satisfied?"

"It's not exactly a role that suits me," she said.

"I think you're doing fine," he told her as they drove along the shore road.

She stared off into the darkness to the right. "Somehow I think you're on the wrong track. I don't think Sheila murdered Helen."

"Why not?"

"I don't see her as a murderess."

"You don't know her."

"Maybe not," Kim said. "But she must have realized that you would never marry a girl like Helen—that in the end you'd likely turn back to her."

Johnny admitted, "What you say is true, but I don't think she was sure of it. She panicked and so she shoved Helen over the side. Perhaps it wasn't even premeditated. She saw Helen drunk, and in a moment of jealous hatred, pushed her. It would just take a second. She may even have convinced herself it was an accident."

"Why her continual harping on the fact she has seen Helen's ghost?"

"That's to torment me," Johnny said. "She still can't forgive me for playing around. She'll be at the dance tonight, and my guess is she'll start sniping at you."

Kim sighed. "Yes. I keep forgetting I'm now her great love rival."

Johnny said, "Just at a time when I'm starting to think you're ideal in the role, I think I'm really beginning to fall in love with you."

This alarmed her. She said, "You were very definite that you didn't care for me in Boston."

"That was Boston and this is Dark Harbor," he said lightly.

"Don't complicate things anymore," she begged him.

Within a few minutes they drove into the huge asphalt parking lot of the Dark Harbor Yacht Club. The lot was nearly filled with cars and the two-story white clubhouse overlooking the ocean was brightly lighted. From inside, the sound of an excellent dance band could be heard.

"I'd have driven you to the door," Johnny said, "but it's only a short distance and I preferred to be with you when you made your entrance."

"This is fine," she said as they approached the steps of the club veranda. There were a half-dozen couples standing on the veranda with its tall, round pillars. And, as she drew near them, she gave a startled gasp. Standing by the entrance to the club was Bill Griffith!

CHAPTER NINE

Kim could not restrain an excited cry. "Bill!"

The young man's good-natured face showed his delight at seeing her. He said, "Well, at least you remember me. That's something."

They kissed as Johnny stood by looking somewhat less than happy. And then Johnny asked, "How did you get over here, Griffith?" When they had worked in Boston together he'd called the young stage manager by his first name, but now he was being deliberately more aloof it seemed.

Bill turned to the sullen Johnny and quite pleasantly said, "A friend of mine leads the orchestra which your club hired for this dance. He invited me to come over with him as soloist. I sing a bit, if you remember. I've done some musicals."

Johnny frowned. "I never heard of you doing anything but stage-managing."

"My dark past," Bill smiled. "I was an actor first. When I had the invitation, I decided it would be a chance to come over and perhaps see Kim."

"I'm so glad you decided to come!" Kim said happily.

Bill turned to her again. "If I hadn't found you here, I would have driven to Craig House between my appearances with the band and looked for you."

Kim glanced at Johnny and said, "Isn't it fun? Our being together again, like this."

"Yes," he said without enthusiasm. And rather surlily, he told Bill, "We'll see you later. Right now we have to go in."

"Sure," Bill said. And with a smile he asked Kim, "Save

some dances for me. I want to have a talk with you."

"I will," she promised.

Johnny almost roughly led her on in by the arm and she could sense his taut reaction to Bill's return. But at the same time she felt a great relief in seeing the young stage manager again. She wanted badly to talk with him though she knew she dare not tell him all she had discovered since coming to Dark Harbor.

Johnny paused to pay their admission to the dance, and they moved into the ballroom of the rambling white building fronting on the ocean. The band was already playing on a bandstand at one end of the room, and there was a long bar crowded with couples at the other. The rafters of the room had been hung with colored strips of crepe paper bunting, and there were a number of flags of the various yacht clubs strung up at intervals. A good number of couples were dancing to the pleasant music as Johnny led her out on the floor.

As they began to dance, he said, "Did you know Bill Griffith was coming here tonight?"

"How could I have?" she asked in surprise.

The handsome star looked sullen as they moved around the floor. "It seems like almost too much of a coincidence!"

"I don't know what you mean!" was her protest. "Bill explained that he came to sing with the band and hoped to see me. There's nothing mysterious about that."

"He's working at that theater on the Cape. How did he get away?"

"You know he always gets at least one night a week off," she reminded him. "I think you're being silly in your attitude."

Johnny scowled. "I don't like him here spoiling my evening."

"Surely his having a dance or two with me won't do that," she protested. "You wouldn't want to dance with me all evening in any case."

Johnny persisted. "I can't help thinking this was arranged between you two!"

"Silly!" she said. "I didn't know until the last moment that there was a dance or that you were taking me."

This seemed to placate him a little, but she could tell he was still definitely suspicious—or was it uneasy? It was hard to say. They were still dancing when Bill took the stand to sing with the band. He did very well, and there was mild applause when he finished. Kim noted that Johnny conspicuously avoided taking part in this.

The music ended for a brief period, and Johnny went to the bar to get drinks for them. She was left standing alone. As she waited for Johnny's return, she saw that Bill was busy talking to the orchestra leader on the stand. She wondered when she would have a chance to talk with him and how to manage it without enraging Johnny.

Then she saw Sheila, resplendent in a filmy pale blue dress studded with sparkling white rhinestones coming across the room in her direction. She was on the arm of a tall white-haired man with a battered brick-red face which must have once been handsome, but those features were now blurred by too many years of heavy drinking.

Sheila halted and smiled at her and said, "Kim, this is my father."

Shyly Kim said, "I'm happy to meet you, Mr. Moore."

The big man had a genial, alcoholic vagueness about him as he smiled and told her, "My daughter's girlfriends continue to be prettier with every meeting."

Sheila gave a small tinkle of laughter and said, "You see how gallant he can be?"

Johnny returned with drinks at this moment and there was general conversation between them all. Kim felt a number of eyes in the room were on them. She also sensed that though the talk they were having was pleasantly animated, there was a tenseness underlying it all.

They'd been talking only a short time when the music began again and Bill suddenly appeared and asked her to dance. Johnny looked as if he might be going to show some objection, but Sheila quickly caught him by the arm and reminded him that this was a favorite number of theirs.

As Bill began dancing with Kim he said wryly, "I don't think Johnny is very happy to see me."

"You mustn't mind him," she said.

"He's a little rough to take," Bill said. "You and I were friends long before he came along."

"I know."

Bill eyed her solicitously. "You look pale and tired, rather than being rested for your time over here. Is something wrong?"

"Not really. I'm anxious to get back to work."

Bill grimaced. "You'll never find work over here."

"I realize that, but Johnny has a possible job coming up at Falmouth. If he gets it, he thinks he can sell me in the package as well."

"Good," Bill said. "And if that doesn't happen, what then?"

"I don't know," she said with a tiny sigh.

"You're not going to stay here? I wondered about your coming here in the first place!"

She managed a wan smile. "It's been a nice holiday."

"You don't show the benefits. Has Johnny tried to play the great lover for your benefit?"

"Nothing like that!" she protested.

"I was afraid he'd try to take advantage of your being his guest," Bill said candidly. "I can't see how you can enjoy yourself at Craig House. He's so tense all the time."

"That is wearying," she said.

The music ended and Bill suggested, "Let's go out on the veranda for a moment."

She left the dance floor, hand in hand with him, and they made their exit through one of the series of french doors which opened from the ballroom onto the veranda, which received its only light through the curtained french windows. Outside, the air was cool and tangy with the smell of the ocean. They strolled over by the wooden railing which overlooked the ocean. In the distance were the colored markers of beacons and pleasure craft.

Bill still held her hand and now as he gazed at her tenderly he took her in his arms and drew her to him for a long, ardent kiss. When he released her, he murmured, "I've missed you! Missed you so much!"

"I've missed you, Bill," she whispered staring up at his friendly, good-looking face.

"What really is holding you here?" he worried.

She hesitated. "I can't tell you everything, Bill. It's very mixed up."

"I gather that," he said dryly.

"There are some things I have to find out," she said. "As soon as I do, I'm going to leave."

"What sort of things?"

She pressed close to him and stared out at the ocean, not wanting him to study her face. She said tautly, "Things happened before I came here. I have somehow been involved with them. Now I don't feel that I can leave without discovering what they mean."

"You're not really telling me anything," Bill grumbled.

"I can't now," she said. "But when it is over I will."

He held her so that he could look into her face again and frowning, asked her, "The thing I must know is whether all this business places you in any sort of danger?"

"Nothing that you should worry about," she said.

He stared at her. "It's not a convincing performance. I find myself doubting you."

"Don't let's talk about it anymore," she pleaded. "We'd best go inside. Johnny will notice I'm missing and will be getting angry."

"Are you so afraid of him?"

"No."

"Or so answerable to him for your actions?"

"No!" she said. "I just don't want to give him any excuse for misbehaving."

"If you remember, he doesn't need much excuse," Bill said with a grim smile.

"We'll go back inside and I'll meet you later."

"When and where?"

She glanced at her wristwatch. "Out here at eleven-thirty? Is that all right with you?"

"I'll see that it is," Bill said. "I'll meet you right here."

"Are you going back tonight?"

Bill said, "Yes. The band is taking a late ferry back. I have to be at the theater early in the morning. But I'm going to worry about you."

"You mustn't!" she told him as they rejoined the dancers in the ballroom.

Bill left her to join the band and do some more singing. She was alone for a few minutes and saw Irma dancing by in the arms of an attentive Jim Blake. Johnny's sister and the suave young lawyer with the thin mustache smiled at her, and she felt an instant dislike for the devious Jim. She realized that she had sensed something sinister about him from the start and hadn't been able to decide what it was.

Dr. Taylor's account of Helen Walsh's pregnancy by the young lawyer had brought it all into focus. She found herself again speculating whether it had been a desperate Jim Blake who had shoved a drunken Helen overboard the night of the cruise. It appeared he was coldly ambitious enough to commit any crime to share the Craig fortune.

She was lost in these thoughts when an irate Johnny came across the dimly lighted ballroom to join her and say, "You were gone long enough!"

"I don't know what you mean," she argued. "I've been here and on the veranda the whole time."

"Off doing the heavy love bit with your old friend," Johnny said with sarcasm.

"If you're going to be like that!" she protested.

"What do you expect?" Johnny demanded. "I'm jealous!"

"You have no right to be," she said. "And you've had Sheila to keep you company."

Johnny glowered at this. "That's another thing. Your whole reason for being here is to protect me from her! You're not doing much of a job tonight!"

"Sorry," she said. "I'm beginning to think it's a job I can well do without."

"Is Griffith trying to get you to leave?"

"What if he is?"

"I thought he would be," Johnny said grimly. "You can't do it! You have a contract with me!"

She smiled scornfully. "I'd hardly call it that. Anyway, you have no need to worry. I told him I wasn't going to leave."

Somewhat placated by her words, Johnny asked, "How am I to believe that?"

"You have to trust me," she replied. "Let's dance again."

Without much enthusiasm Johnny took her out on the floor once again. And when they had danced for a little, Derek Mills came over and asked her to join him in a waltz. The museum director looked especially handsome in his white jacket and black tie.

As they danced, Derek said, "Are you enjoying yourself?"

She stared up at him. "Why do you ask?"

"Johnny seems in such a bad humor and you are so tense," he said.

"I had a friend turn up unexpectedly," she explained. "Johnny has chosen to resent it."

"That's in character," Derek said as they waltzed. "I recall he created a drunken scene the night of the dance last year. Then it was he and Helen who quarreled."

"An old story for him," she said. "Was Sheila here that night?"

"Yes. She enjoyed it all from the sidelines. Then when Johnny stalked away from Helen, it was Sheila who joined him. They left together."

"Tonight I'm the other party," she said bitterly.

"You talked with Dr. Taylor?" Derek asked.

"Yes."

"Then you know what I meant when I said Johnny didn't have all the facts."

"Yes," she said. "I've had a funny feeling about Jim Blake from the start. Now it makes sense."

"He's here with Irma and enjoying himself," Derek Mills said.

"So I noticed," Kim said. "I think Dr. Taylor ought to have told the police what he told me."

"I doubt if it would do any good," Derek Mills said. "Still, I have urged him to do that very thing."

The waltz ended and Derek escorted her back to Johnny.

She remained with him until it was nearly eleven-thirty. Then she made an excuse to leave and freshen up. And when she came from the ladies room, she went directly to the veranda rather than returning to Johnny. She was extremely nervous as she stood by the wooden railing.

The dark veranda seemed to be completely deserted. She glanced up and down its long length and saw no one. The air had changed and it was strangely humid. There seemed to be no breeze. She stared out at the ocean with its dots of lights marking the pleasure craft. And once again she thought of that midnight cruise when Helen Walsh had vanished. This was accompanied by her vision of that phantom figure in the sparkling sheath dress, dripping wet from the sea and draped with seaweed! It was a terrifying picture, and she felt herself cold with fear.

Then she heard a movement from behind her. An almost furtive movement. She turned with a start to see the blurred figure of Jim Blake standing there in the shadows. He said, "They're looking for you."

She regained some of her poise as she replied, "You mean Johnny is looking for me?"

"Yes. Irma asked me to help."

"I felt I needed some air," she said.

"Oh?" There was a mocking quality in his voice.

She stared out at the ocean again in time to see some heat lightning flash across the dark sky. Tautly, she said, "I think there is going to be a storm."

"Could be," Jim Blake agreed. "It's that sort of night. What we don't want is a storm *inside*."

Kim turned to see his mocking smile. "What do you mean by that?"

"Let's not spar with words," the young lawyer said. "I know you have a friend here. I've seen you with him."

Kim said, "What about it?"

"Johnny doesn't like it," Jim Blake warned her. "He's not beyond starting a row here. The Craigs don't like that sort of scene or any trouble."

She smiled sarcastically. "I'd expect they'd be used to it by now!"

"If you know what's good for you, don't taunt Johnny too much," the man standing beside her in the darkness warned.

"What business is it of yours?" she demanded sharply.

"I'm trying to be a friend," he said. "I know the Craigs. If you intend to marry Johnny, you'd better watch your step. You can't expect to share all that money too easily."

"Who would know that better than you?" she asked bitterly.

Jim Blake gave a small gasp. In a hard voice, he asked, "Just what does that mean?"

"I'll let you judge," was her reply.

She was immediately conscious of the anger radiating from the slim young man as he stood there with clenched hands. It was fortunate that at that moment Bill Griffith came out on the veranda as they'd planned. Jim Blake gave Bill a sour look and stalked off inside.

Bill gave her a questioning glance. "Who was that and what has he against me?"

She smiled wanly. "He's not anyone important. Don't give it a thought."

"How can you stand this place?" he wanted to know. "I've never seen such a collection of weirdos!"

"Don't worry about it," Kim said.

Bill took her in his arms again. "I'm worried about you."
"I'll survive."

"You'd better," he said. "Promise me you'll get out of

here whether that job turns up at Falmouth or not."

"All right," she said.

"You mean it?" he persisted.

"Yes," she nodded. "I hope to leave here within a few days."

"And you'll break off this thing with Johnny?"

"That will be part of it."

Bill looked worried. "You knew from the start he was bad news. I can't guess how you managed to get yourself so involved with him."

"A long story. You'll hear it one day."

"I want to," Bill said and again he kissed her tenderly. And though she had never considered herself in love with Bill, she found herself responding to his caresses with a warmth which startled her.

She looked up at him lovingly and wondered if her true feeling hadn't been suddenly revealed. She knew only that she had never responded to Johnny in this fashion. She said, "We mustn't stay out here too long."

"I can't," Bill said. "I have to sing a few choruses and then the dance will be over. I'll be leaving. I may not have a chance to see you again."

"I'll see you soon," she promised.

"Come to me when you leave here," he said.

"I'll phone you before I leave," she told him. "I have the theater's phone number."

"If I'm not there, they can always reach me," Bill told her. "And watch out for Johnny. I don't trust him!"

"I know," she said.

His lips found hers again. The embrace was as sweet as it was brief. Then, with an almost anguished air, the young man went back inside, leaving her alone by the veranda railing. The heat lightning flashed across the dark sky again, and she realized that it was coming with more frequency.

In the eerie silence of the dark veranda, the orchestra sounded in the distance. And then there was a more urgent sound of one of the french doors opening close behind her. She glanced up to see Sheila sauntering out to her.

"So this is where you are!" Sheila said.

"Yes," she answered, not sure of the other girl's mood.

"I saw your friend come back inside just now," Sheila said with a knowing air.

"Oh?"

"Johnny is in a rage. Better watch out," Sheila taunted her with a smile.

"I don't know what you're talking about," Kim said.

"I'm sure you do," Sheila went on mocking. "I think this other fellow is much more your type. You're being sensible."

"Thank you," Kim said ironically.

Sheila went on in her tormenting fashion, "I intend to marry Johnny anyway. So the sooner you break with him the better."

"How can you be so sure of him?"

"I am."

"Whether I intend to marry Johnny or not, I doubt that you ever will," Kim told the black-haired girl.

Sheila gave a small laugh. "That shows how much you know! You're a stranger to Dark Harbor and its people. You don't have any idea what has gone on here or what will happen!"

Kim said, "I have an idea of what happened to Helen Walsh. No wonder you see her ghost since the poor girl was surely murdered."

Sheila lost her poise and stared at Kim wordlessly for a moment. Then she gasped, "How dare you say a thing like that?"

"Because I believe it. Perhaps your ghostly visions are due to a guilty conscience."

The other girl continued to appear shocked. She said, "You can get yourself into great trouble saying things like that!"

"I'm willing to risk that," Kim said defiantly.

"You're going just a little too far," Sheila said with hatred in her tone.

"I wonder," Kim said, satisfied that she'd upset the other girl.

The french doors opened again. This time Johnny came out. He glanced at them both and said to Kim, "It's the last dance. I've been looking for you." And he led her out into the ballroom, leaving Sheila there staring after them angrily.

On the dance floor Kim looked up at the handsome young star and said, "You weren't very polite. You didn't even speak to Sheila out there."

"I didn't want to," he replied.

"You must want her to hate us both," she said.

"I have come to a point," Johnny said bitterly, "where I don't care what she thinks."

"Where is her father?" she asked.

"Probably at the bar, drunk. That's where he usually winds up. She'll have to drive him home."

"Not very pleasant for her," Kim said.

"That's her affair," was Johnny's curt comment.

At that moment Bill sang his last chorus of the evening for the good-night waltz. She smiled at him as they danced by and he waved in return. For a moment some of the tension left her and she felt almost happy. Then the pressures closed in again. When the music ended Johnny led her away without giving her any chance to speak to Bill again.

In the car on the way home Johnny said, "I don't want you

to see that Griffith anymore."

"What's wrong with Bill?" she asked.

"He acts as if he owns you!"

"You simply imagine that!" she protested.

"I know him," Johnny said grimly. "And I don't want to play games over you with him. I'm in love with you and I want to marry you."

"You don't really mean that," she accused him.

He glanced at her from the wheel. "Why do you say that?"

"I think I know you," she said, studying him in the near darkness of the car's front seat. "You care more for yourself than anyone else. All actors have a great ego, but you are the most egotistical one I've ever met."

"Thanks!" Johnny said bitterly.

"I'm trying to be your friend," she said. "I think you should face up to yourself honestly."

"If I need a psychiatrist I can find one," he jeered. "I don't need amateur ones like you."

"Professional help might be good for you," she said.

He drove on much too fast for the dark narrow road as he vented his anger on his driving. He said, "Are you trying to say I'm crazy?"

"No. But you are opinionated and egotistical to a dangerous point," she said. "It has even harmed your career."

"I've done well enough!"

"Only because of your great talent," she said. "Otherwise you'd have been dropped long ago. And you've been most unfair to Sheila."

"Don't start that!"

"She really loves you."

"Who cares?"

Kim said, "She says she means to marry you."

He glanced at her briefly again. "Did she tell you that?"

"Yes. She seems certain of it."

"She's wrong!"

"I wonder," she said. "Just as I wonder about her seeing the ghost of Helen Walsh. So strange that she's the only one who sees it."

"I told you why," he said. "Sheila murdered Helen."

"I question that."

"How can you?"

"I think some man did it," Kim said.

They had reached the parking space by Craig House and he shut off the engine of the big car and stared at her in the shadows. "Why do you think a man did it?"

"Because she knew a number of men. It's possible she may have made an enemy of one of them."

Johnny shook his head. "You're on the wrong track."

"I wonder," she said.

They got out of the car to the accompaniment of thunder and lightning. The storm seemed to be approaching rapidly. They went inside the gloom of the old mansion and Johnny accompanied her up the stairway to the door of her room.

"We're likely to have a bad storm," he told her.

"I know," she said with a tiny shudder. "I hate electrical storms."

He said, "We could stay downstairs and talk awhile."

The prospect didn't please her. She said, "No. I'm tired. I'm going to bed. The storm may pass over."

Johnny was studying her intently. "You were beautiful tonight. The most beautiful girl there!"

"That's flattery," she protested. "Sheila was lovely and so was your sister Irma."

Johnny shrugged. "Irma is my sister. You don't notice your sister as an attractive female."

"Why not?"

"Take too long to explain," Johnny said. He kissed her briefly and she went inside.

Kim carefully bolted the door behind her and then crossed the big room to glance out the window. It was strangely dark out there. The lighthouse beam from Gull's Point stood out strongly against the blackness. There were none of the usual dots of colored lights out on the water. Most of the small craft had apparently been warned of an approaching storm and headed in to safe harbor.

She remained at the window until the lightning came again. This time it was very sharp and flooded the sky momentarily with a vivid bluish white. She turned from the window, realizing that she was trembling. The ordeal of the evening was already telling on her. Slowly she went about preparing for bed.

Thunder sounded close and made her wonder and worry about Bill. He and the other members of the orchestra were taking a late-night ferry trip back to the mainland. It could be a rough trip if the storm amounted to anything. Perhaps the crossing might be postponed or even cancelled.

She had not dared to confide in Bill, and yet he seemed to be aware of her dangerous position. He had urged her to leave Dark Harbor and the island. And she knew he was right. The longer she remained, the more involved she became in the sinister tragedy of the drowning of Helen Walsh. She wished she could flee the island and forget all about it. But she knew that if she left without making an effort to get to the bottom of the mystery, it would haunt her forever.

Johnny insisted that Sheila was the murderer. But Sheila had not reacted as one might have expected when she'd talked to her very directly about the tragedy. It could be that Dr. Taylor was correct in his suspicions.

More than ever, it now seemed possible that a frantic Jim

Blake had shoved the drunken and pregnant girl overboard to stop her from telling Irma all the facts. Kim knew that when she'd practically accused him of the murder, he had reacted strongly. As he'd walked away, there had been a guilty air about him. But how could one possibly prove his guilt?

This was the big question. She settled into bed as another flash of lightning lit up the dark room. Closing her eyes, she tried to ignore the storm. She worried about Sheila and felt she ought to have a frank discussion with her. She wanted to tell Sheila that she didn't love Johnny and would never try to marry him. This should satisfy Sheila. In turn, she would seek Sheila's help in finding out who had been responsible for Helen Walsh's drowning. She felt certain the black-haired girl knew more than she was willing to reveal.

The thunder crashed outside and Kim sat up in bed with a frightened expression on her attractive face. The storm seemed close at hand now. And as if to underlie this, there came a deluge of rain lashed by a high wind. The rain pounded against her windows and from somewhere outside she heard a shutter banging.

The clatter of the shutter was like a ghostly knocking. Chill terror coursed down Kim's spine. She tried not to think of the ghost, but the specter kept forcing itself on her. She could see the dripping wet figure in the shining sequined dress. Helen's body had not been found! And on this stormy night her bodily remains must be lurking somewhere in the depths of the turmoil of the ocean.

Again the thunder came sharply with the blue lightning. She moaned and covered her ears with her hands. Outside the wind and rain lashed the old mansion relentlessly. It seemed that all the hatred and anger present in the old house had been released in the storm.

She let her hands drop from her ears and debated leaving

her room and going downstairs. Perhaps some of the others might have been awakened by the storm and would be down there. Company would be most welcome on this awful night. But almost at once she knew that she dare not leave her room at this hour. She was too frightened of what might be lurking out there in the shadows of the corridor.

A sharp stab of terror went through her as she thought she heard a moaning sound from that other room! The room to which the mad old Grace had been consigned and which was only separated from hers by a thin door! Thoughts of the possibility of the old madwoman still being in there and in a state of violence agitated by the storm came to torment her!

Still sitting up in bed, she listened intently for some sound from that room of mystery again. But there was only silence. The lightning and thunder seemed just outside her windows now. She shuddered at their impact. And she wondered how long the storm might go on and how long she could endure it.

The burst of heavy rain came again, and with it the wind. It set the loose shutter clattering in ghostly fashion once more. It was a vicious sequence of events. And then she caught her breath in something like a sob. For there was now another pounding, aside from the shutter. It seemed that someone was pounding on the other side of the door separating her room from the one occupied so long by the madwoman!

Kim drew back against the pillows as the thunder and lightning came again fiercely and at the same instant the door between her room and that of Aunt Grace sprang open to reveal the phantom figure of the drowned Helen Walsh standing in the middle of that other room!

CHAPTER TEN

Kim could not restrain a terrified scream. Then she collapsed on the bed.

She was brought to a kind of muddled consciousness by the sound of someone pounding on the hall door and calling out her name in a frenzied manner. Slowly she lifted herself up and at once memory of that terror returned and she let her eyes dart quickly to the door which had sprung open to reveal the ghost. The door was now closed, as usual, and the storm had abated. The sound of thunder was distant and the lightning weak.

Her name was called again and the pounding continued. She weakly swung her feet off the bed and found her slippers. Then she put on the robe which she always left there and made her way to the door, drew back the bolt, and opened it.

Standing in the corridor was Stephen Craig in bathrobe and pajamas. His white hair was rumpled and he looked less than his usual aristocratic self. In a disturbed voice, he asked her, "What was wrong in there? I was passing by your door and I heard the most dreadful screams."

Leaning weakly against the door frame, she said, "I'm sorry. I had a bad scare."

"The storm?"

"Something more than that."

"Something more than that?" the old man stared at her in an incredulous fashion.

"Yes," she said, gazing at him forlornly. "The door to the next room sprang open and I saw a figure."

Stephen Craig looked skeptical. "The door to the locked room?"

"Yes."

"You have to be mistaken," he declared at once. "There is never anyone in that room!"

"The door sprang open as the lightning flashed," she told him. "I saw something standing there."

"It can't be!" Stephen Craig said almost angrily.

"I screamed and fainted."

He frowned at her. "Let me see that door," he said. And he strode into the room and crossed to the door and roughly twisted the handle. The door would not open. He turned to her. "What about that? The door is locked!"

"I can't help it," she said weakly. "I saw what I saw!"

The white-haired man looked impatient. "You've been having hysterics, young lady!"

"No!"

He raised a protesting hand. "No reason for you to be ashamed. The storm was frightful. That is why I was up and about. I heard a shutter clattering and went to see if I could stop it."

"I really saw the door open and saw a ghost," Kim insisted.

"That storm upset you," Johnny's father went on tolerantly. "We won't worry anymore about it. Go to bed and forget it happened. Depend on me not to tell the others."

She stared at him. "You think I imagined it all?"

"Or dreamed it," the old man said. "What difference does it make?"

She said, "The fact that door is locked now doesn't prove anything. It could have been open."

Stephen Craig said, "I only know it's locked now. Good night, Miss Rice. I suggest you go back to bed and clear your mind of all such thoughts. It's the best way to insure sleep." And with a nod to her, he left.

Kim switched on the overhead lights in her room and closed the door after him. Her heart was still pounding from the eerie experience she'd had. But she was not surprised that the staid Mr. Craig had refused to listen to her story. Yet she knew that this time it had not been imagination or hysterics. The door of the room *had* sprung open and she had seen what appeared to be the phantom figure of Helen Walsh.

Now she glanced towards the door apprehensively and after a moment summoned the courage to cross to the door and try the knob herself. Stephen Craig bad been correct in at least one thing: the knob refused to turn. She could only surmise that it had been locked again on the other side. But whose hand could have locked it?

It was some time before she returned to bed. Then she left the lights on and tried to seek sleep. When sleep did come, it was a light, uneasy one in which she dreamed of the ghost with seaweed draped across a lovely face! The slim body in its sequined evening gown from which the seawater dripped! The icy hands reached out to grip her in a chill embrace!

She screamed and woke again. She was badly upset even though she knew that it had been a nightmare. She sat up in bed trembling, with her eyes fixed on that door. She was still tormented by a desire to know what might lie behind it. What secret did the locked room hold? She had noticed the hasty and almost feverish reaction of Stephen's father when she had mentioned the room to him. Was there a madwoman in there still, warning free in the dark hours to terrorize them all?

Kim shut her eyes and again dozed off. This time she had a dream about Sheila. She thought she was walking with the lovely black-haired girl along the cliffs when suddenly Jim Blake appeared and came towards them with his thin face distorted by hatred. The young man with the mustache charged at Sheila and hurled her over the cliffs. Sheila screamed and screamed, and again Kim came awake.

By now it was dawn. She rested fitfully until it was time to get up for breakfast. It was a gray, foggy morning and matched her mood exactly. She washed and dressed slowly and saw by the mirror that her pale, drawn face bore witness to the ordeal of the night. She determined to tell Johnny about her experience as soon as she saw him. And she also thought she would seek out Derek Mills and ask his advice.

She touched up her pale cheeks with some rouge and then made her way downstairs. The moment she reached the bottom of the stairway, she knew something had happened to upset the Craigs. She saw Johnny standing with his mother and father in a solemn conclave.

Slowly she crossed over to them and met their strained silence with the question: "Has something happened?"

Johnny nodded, his handsome face shadowed. He said, "Yes. There's been a dreadful accident."

"Though not altogether surprising," his mother said in a prim if subdued fashion.

Stephen Craig gave his wife a frown. "We are not to judge," he reminded her.

Johnny sighed and told Kim, "Prepare yourself for a shock."

She felt frightened without knowing why. She asked, "What?"

"Sheila is dead," he said tautly.

"Sheila!" she exclaimed in disbelief.

"It is hard to realize," he agreed.

"But I was talking to her late last night," Kim said.

"I know," Johnny sighed.

Stephen Craig said stiffly, "It is doubly tragic when the

dead person is so young."

"Her father must be stricken by his share in it," Johnny's mother said grimly.

Tears filled Kim's eyes. She had known Sheila only a brief time, and there had been bitter arguments between them, but it did not seem right that the vivacious girl should now be dead.

She said, "I feel weak. I'm going to sit down a moment."

"Do," Johnny urged and he led her to the nearest hall chair.

After she'd been seated a moment, she asked, "What caused her death?"

"The gardener found her in the garage with the door locked and the car still running. She'd apparently let her drunken father out at the front door and he'd gone inside by himself. Then she used the electric control in the car to open the garage door and after she'd driven in closed it after her by the same control. She would normally have turned off the engine and gotten out of the car and gone into the house by the side door."

"But she didn't do that?"

"No," Johnny said. "She must have dropped off to sleep as soon as she closed the door. The engine kept running and the carbon monoxide killed her. She was found slumped over the wheel."

"Wouldn't her father miss her and look for her?" Kim asked.

"Too drunk. He went straight up to bed and was asleep in a few minutes," the handsome star said.

"Horrible!" Kim said. "I didn't think she'd been drinking all that much. She seemed quite sober when I talked with her."

"She was a deceptive drinker," Johnny said. "She

wouldn't show anything at all, and then suddenly it would hit her. I'd say that was what happened last night."

"I still can't believe it," she said, conscious again that Johnny's parents were in the background.

Stephen Craig said, "This will finish Sheila's father. He's been gradually drinking himself to death, and this will hasten it."

"No question of that," Johnny's mother agreed.

Kim was aware of a missing member of the family. She asked, "Where is Irma?"

"My sister and Jim Blake went over to see if they could be of any help," Johnny said.

Kim recalled, "I thought Sheila's father had a long-time feud with Jim Blake."

"I don't think that would matter at a time like this," Johnny said.

"No, of course not," she agreed. "One feels so powerless."

"She's dead and there's nothing to be done about it," Johnny said. "You don't want to be ill. Better go in and have some breakfast."

"I don't feel like anything," she protested.

"You still need something," he said.

After some more urging she went in to the dining room, but all she could manage was some coffee. After that she went to the living room and to her relief found Johnny standing somberly by the big bay windows, alone.

He glanced at her as she came into the room. "Feeling better?" he asked.

"Not much," she said.

"I know," he sighed. And again he stared out the big windows at the fog-shrouded garden outside.

She stood by him and said, "It's all so hard to believe. She was so sure she would marry you."

"Don't remind me of that!" he protested, still staring out at the fog.

"But you couldn't help being impressed by her insistence," Kim said. "She never seemed to doubt you'd marry her."

"She was wrong."

"She didn't think so. And I am here because of her. You had me come here to stand between you two."

"I needed you."

"I feel responsible for what happened in a way," Kim went on brokenly. "She was drinking because I was there, a threat to her."

Johnny turned to her urgently. "Don't get that in your head!"

"I think there is something in it. I had strange dreams last night."

He stared at her. "What sort of dreams?"

"I had two. First, I was sure the door leading to the room next to mine sprang open and I saw the figure of the ghost of Helen Walsh!"

"You've had that sort of dream before!" Johnny said curtly.

"The next one was different. In it Sheila was hurled over the cliffs and her screams woke me up!" Kim said, gazing at him in awe at the remembrance of it.

He showed impatience. "How can that have any meaning?"

In a voice with a tremor in it, she said, "Maybe the screams I heard were her screams when she was actually dying. They came to me in the middle of the night."

"Rot!" Johnny said with scorn. "She slept into her death. There were no screams."

"How can you know?"

"From the way she was discovered."

Kim shook her head. "I still somehow feel guilty."

Johnny took her by the arm and gazed at her with grim eyes. "Look! Don't be such a little fool!"

"Why do you say that?"

"Because of the sort of person Sheila was. Remember?"

She winced at the pain he was causing her by his fierce hold on her arms. "What do you mean?"

"Don't forget Sheila was probably a murderess!"

"I never really could make myself believe that."

"I was there that night," he said. "I'm almost as sure as if I had actually seen her shove Helen overboard!"

"It's conjecture!"

"No," he went on. "I think that Sheila was a suicide. That she probably took something in her drink and deliberately brought on her own death by remaining in that car with the motor running."

Her eyes widened. "If that is so, the police will find out about it."

"Probably," he said. "They were called and must be there now."

Kim tried to match it all. "If she were guilty, she might have decided to take her life."

"That's what I've been trying to make you understand."

"I don't even want to think about it," she said unhappily.

He released her arms. "I had to make you see that you were in no way to blame."

"Poor girl!" she said.

"I think you should go to your room and take some sort of sedative," he advised. "Try and rest a little. You look worn out."

She took his advice. Fortunately she had a small vial of sleeping pills which had been given to her once during a play's run when she'd been troubled with insomnia. She'd recovered from the annoyance when the play closed. Now she had them to use again. She took one with a glass of water and stretched out on her bed. Sleep came almost at once.

She had no idea how long she slept, but when she woke up Irma Craig was standing at her bedside staring down at her. Johnny's pretty sister looked worried.

Irma said, "I was beginning to think something was wrong with you."

She raised herself on an elbow. "I took a sleeping pill."

"Oh?" Irma looked grim.

"What went on over there?" Kim asked, referring to what had gone on at the Moore house.

Irma said, "I just came back a half-hour ago. I had to sit with Sheila's father. He's in a terrible state, drinking every minute."

"He's still drinking after what happened?"

"Because of it. Of course, he blames himself and he is partly right."

"What did the police find?" Kim asked.

Irma crossed to an easy chair and slumped down in it. She gave Kim a listless glance. "Sheila had taken some drugs as well as having had too much to drink."

Kim's eyebrows raised. "You're sure?"

The other girl nodded. "The police came while I was there. Very official they were. The had a report of the autopsy to offer Mr. Moore."

"And you heard it?"

"I had to remain to support the grieving father," Irma said with disgust. "He could barely sit up let alone listen to them."

"Do you think he even understood what they told him?"

"I doubt it."

"That's tragic!"

"It's all tragic," Irma said in a dull voice. "She either took some sleeping pills deliberately or by accident."

"How could she do it by accident?"

"She also had pep pills in her purse. She might have gotten the two mixed since she was drinking."

Kim admitted, "I hadn't thought of that."

"The police claim it happens pretty often," she said. "They told the bereaved father that it was an accident and that no one should be blamed."

"Small comfort."

Irma nodded. "I know. Anyway, that's the end of Sheila. Accidental death."

"She was so alive when I talked with her last night," Kim recalled.

"I saw her," Irma said. "And I'm sure, by the way she was acting, she was terribly jealous of you and Johnny."

Kim said, "I shall always feel badly about that."

"Why?"

"It was so needless," Kim said.

"That's not exactly true, is it?" Irma questioned her.

"Why do you say that?"

The other girl shrugged. "You came here as Johnny's fiancée. Certainly Sheila had to resent you!"

"But I'm not in love with Johnny!" she protested.

Irma showed surprise. "Yet you plan to marry him?"

"That's another story," she said. "I can't talk about it now. Johnny will explain to you at his leisure."

"I need no explanation," Irma said disconsolately. "I expect yours is another love match like mine and Jim Blake's!"

She stared at the other girl. "I have always thought you and Jim were deeply in love!"

Irma looked scornful. "Jim is in love, all right. In love with my money!"

"What?"

"The money I will one day inherit," the other girl went on bitterly. "I know that's what he really cares for. And I suppose you care for Johnny because of his money and fame. Well, that's the way of the world, I guess!"

"You mustn't be so bitter!" Kim protested.

"I'm not bitter," Irma said. "I accept. And after seeing Sheila the way I did this morning, nothing much shocks me anymore. Nothing seems to matter."

Kim was on her feet by the other girl's chair. She said, "I want you to know that you're wrong about me, and probably about a lot of other things."

"Let's not worry about it now," Irma said wearily. "We're alive, and that means we're doing better than Sheila. We ought to be satisfied."

"I still can't think of her as dead," Kim said.

Irma rose with a bleak look on her attractive face. "You'd better get used to the idea." And with that she turned and left the room.

Kim stared after her. In many ways she felt that Irma was the most difficult of all the Craig family to really know. Johnny's sister had managed to keep a protective barrier around her ever since she'd met her. And there had been an oddness in her manner in the way she'd intruded on her while she was asleep and talked of the murder in such a bitter fashion. It made one suspect that she might know about the actions of her fiancé and his role in the drowning of Helen Walsh.

Memory of the other dead girl made her think again of how Johnny had so steadfastly insisted that Sheila had brought about Helen's death. Kim had never believed it and she still felt the lovely black-haired girl innocent of the crime. Still, it was not likely the truth would ever be known now if Sheila had been the guilty one.

A cold shower and a change of dress made Kim feel more alive after the drowsiness left behind by the sleeping pills she'd taken. She went downstairs to join the others at dinner and found them all in a quiet, somber mood. The fog had not moved out, and it was evident that darkness would come early.

Little was said at the table but afterwards Johnny took her aside and in a low voice said, "I have to talk with you."

She glanced at him in mild surprise. "What about?"

"I can't tell you here," he said. "Put on your raincoat and I'll meet you out by the swimming pool."

"All right," she said.

When they met beside the pool about five minutes later, Johnny seemed in a very troubled mood. A frown on his handsome face, he told her, "I couldn't talk frankly in the house."

"I gathered that," she said. His tenseness did not surprise her since she knew Sheila's death must have been a bad shock to him. In spite of his wariness about taking Sheila as his wife, he had undoubtedly cared a lot for her—perhaps more than he'd realized.

He said, "I'm sure she was a suicide."

Her eyebrows lifted. "Why do you say that?"

"Because of the way she talked to me at the dance."

Kim said, "I talked with her as well, and there was no hint of that sort of thing in what she said to me. She kept telling me that no matter what, she was still going to marry you."

"Pure bluff on her part," Johnny said. "The bravado of the loser. I made it clear to her that you and I were in love."

"How could you say that?" she asked sharply.

He shrugged. "I consider it true. Just as I expect we'll marry."

"That's highly unlikely," she said. "But I don't feel in the mood for arguing about it now. At the moment I'd prefer to hear why you think Sheila may have killed herself."

"The end of the line," he said. "She'd murdered Helen Walsh to make sure she had no rival for my affections. Then you came along."

Her eyes met his accusingly. "You *brought* me along."

"I didn't want to marry a murderess."

"Did you tell her that?"

"In so many words."

"That was a dangerous thing to do," Kim said. "You may have been wrong."

His handsome young face was stern. "I think not. The fact she'd taken sleeping pills proves it as far as I'm concerned."

"She was drinking. She may have been confused about the pills."

"Not in my opinion," the young star said. "Her father is taking it badly. I don't look forward to the next couple of days and the funeral."

"It's a time of terrible stress for him," she said. "And more especially since he was too drunk at the time to notice her absence or be any help to her."

"Archer Moore has always been an alcoholic," Johnny said. "With Sheila gone, he'll likely soon drink himself to death."

She stared at Johnny. "The way you say it gives one the impression you hope he will."

"Not at all," he said. "I'm merely stating a fact. Sheila will be in Dark Harbor at the funeral parlor tonight. I'll have to go. I wish you'd come with me."

She didn't relish the prospect. "I rarely go to such places," she said. "What about your father and mother?"

"They'll go on their own," he said.

"And Irma?"

"She and Jim Blake are driving my parents into Dark Harbor," he said. "People will think it funny if you don't go."

She still hesitated and then made a sudden decision. She said, "All right. I'll go with you."

The funeral parlor was on a side street within view of the harbor. The fog was still thick when Kim and Johnny drove up to the drab frame building. A number of cars were parked in front of it, suggesting that a good many mourners had come to pay their last respects.

She felt herself feeling faint as she entered the building on Johnny's arm. Sheila's coffin, banked by floral tributes, rested in the far end of the big room to their right. This room had a wide entrance and Sheila's father was there along with two elderly couples. In a smaller room on the left, the other mourners had gathered to talk in low tones. It was odd, but it somehow reminded Kim of a macabre cocktail party in which there were no drinks served and everyone talked in low voices.

Johnny led her to the casket, and she stood for a moment of grief staring down at the relaxed, pale face of the dead Sheila. She had been laid out in a crimson gown typical of the stylish dresses she regularly wore. The stale sweetness of the flowers made Kim feel ill again. She glanced up at Johnny and saw that he had gone deathly pale and was trembling. Abruptly he gave her a distraught look and turned and hurried out of the room.

To her consternation, Kim found herself alone in the room with the grieving Archer Moore. The two elderly couples had earlier moved on. Now the big white-haired man with the ruined, once-handsome face, licked his parched purplish lips and said, "I thank you for coming, Miss Rice."

Striving to meet the situation, she said, "Sheila and I didn't always see things the same way, but I had respect for her."

Archer Moore teetered ever so slightly and the smell of whiskey was strong on his breath. His brick-red face showed sorrow as he glanced at his daughter's casket and said, "It is strange that you should speak of Sheila in that way. Not more than a week ago, she said almost the same thing to me about you."

This surprised Kim. "She did?"

Archer Moore nodded solemnly. He said, "We had a long talk. Sheila told me that you were no fool. She said she couldn't believe that you were truly interested in Johnny."

Kim believed the old man even though he had clearly been drinking too much. There was a sincerity in his tone that left small doubt in her mind. She said, "Your daughter was right. I think that ultimately she and Johnny would have married. He is badly shaken by her death. You saw how he couldn't bear to remain in the room?"

"Yes, I saw that," Archer Moore said with a puzzled look on his drink-ruined face. "Sheila told me some things that day which I can't recall as I should. She talked very strangely, as if she had some premonition of her death."

"Really?" Kim was at once interested.

"She talked in that way. I think she'd been very bothered by the appearance of that ghost."

"Helen Walsh?"

The white-haired man nodded. "Yes. No one would believe that my daughter really saw the ghost. But I know Sheila wouldn't have said so if she hadn't. It appeared to prey on her mind and make her unduly absorbed with death."

"It would be bound to," she said. "I know the Craig family and others ridiculed her about seeing the phantom figure."

"That was wrong of them," the old man standing facing her complained. "Sheila was worn down by the appearances of the ghost. Little realizing that she was soon to die herself."

"I'm so sorry," Kim said.

"I know," Archer Moore nodded. "I'm trying to remember what she said that day we had our talk. I will later, I'm sure. I'm very confused at the moment."

"Everyone understands," she murmured.

Some other mourners arrived and took Archer Moore's attention from her. Kim was grateful for the chance to escape. As she hurried by the room where the other mourners had assembled, she was conscious of some whisperings and a number of eyes fixed on her with curiosity. She was glad to reach the outside steps and the cold damp air of the foggy night.

Johnny was waiting at the foot of the steps with an air of utter dejection. He apologized, "Sorry I let you down in there. I couldn't remain there looking at Sheila a moment longer."

"It was rather cowardly of you," she reproved him. "You were the one who forced me to come here."

"I know," he said, looking and sounding ashamed.

She couldn't help feeling sorry for him. "I know you cared for Sheila, so you should be forgiven," she said.

"Thank you," he said as they started walking back to the car.

"I didn't see your parents."

"They were in the mourners' room," he said. "They likely thought we would go in for a while. I can't bear that kind of thing. They stay there and talk about Sheila and rehash her death over and over. It's a sort of morbid party occasion."

"The same idea struck me as we went by them," she agreed.

In the car, Johnny asked, "What did Archer Moore say to you?"

"He was really very nice," she said. "Better than I had ever hoped."

"Did he say anything about Sheila's mood the night of her suicide?"

"That hasn't been proven," she objected.

"It never will be," Johnny said, "but I can't think of it otherwise."

She sat beside him in the car's front seat and gave him a troubled glance. "Her father claims that she did really see the ghost and it was the phantom figure which upset her so much."

"Guilty conscience," Johnny said bleakly. "That's why she claimed to see the ghost. She killed Helen and then could not rid herself of the terrible guilt of it. The easy way out was to take her own life."

Kim did not agree with him, but knew it was useless to argue. He had a stubborn streak, and once he'd made up his mind there was no turning it around. So she offered no further comment as he drove her back to Craig House.

The days before the funeral of Sheila were uneventful enough. And so were the two nights. The funeral was delayed until the arrival of Archer Moore's sister from Miami. Ironically enough, his sister didn't remain for the funeral but merely visited the funeral parlor and then took a cab to the small island airport to begin her return journey.

The body was interred in a small cemetery near the cliffside and the ocean. After the service, Johnny's father and mother invited a number of the mourners back to their place for a drink. Archer Moore was invited and declined, but many of the island's best-known citizens agreed to go to Craig House. It was another island custom Johnny assured Kim. It was considered a duty of a close friend of the deceased to provide such refreshments.

Many of the funeral party gathered on the lawn by the gardens of Craig House on that sunny afternoon. Among the guests were Derek Mills and old Captain Zachary Miller, along with Dr. Taylor and his wife. Derek Mills wore a dark blue suit which made him look extremely handsome. He found his way to Kim and they strolled off to one side together.

Derek had a glass in hand as he glanced up at the blue sky with its array of fleecy clouds. "A wonderful afternoon for the funeral," he said.

She gave him a bleak look. "Does it make that much difference to Sheila?"

"I'm afraid not," Derek agreed. He gave her a direct look. "What do you think about her death?"

"What do you mean?"

"The second time a young woman friend of Johnny's has met an accidental death," he said, his brown eyes fixing on hers with a meaningful look.

She felt herself tense. "Are you trying to say you think there may be some link between the two deaths?"

"I mentioned one. Johnny."

"Go on," she said, her tone taut.

"I'm not saying Johnny had anything to do with the deaths."

"I thought you were saying that."

"No," Derek said, glancing over at the group on the distant lawn as if to see whether they were being watched. Then, seeming satisfied that no one had noticed them absent themselves, he gave his full attention to her once again as he said, "Sheila was on that cruise the night Helen went overboard."

"I know."

"You also are aware that Dr. Taylor suspects Jim Blake may have been the one who caused Helen's drowning."

"I know," she agreed with a tiny shudder. "I've worried

about it. Jim Blake does have a sinister side to him. He may truly have been guilty."

"Suppose Sheila saw him shove Helen overboard," Derek Mills said intently. "Wouldn't that mean he'd have to silence her?"

CHAPTER ELEVEN

Kim gasped. "You think that might have happened?"

"It seems possible," Derek replied.

"I suppose so. But how?"

"He could have made sure she was drugged. He'd likely know the type of sleeping pills she'd been taking. Everyone was buying drinks at the dance. He could easily have bought one for her and secretly put the pills in it."

"And then what?"

"After that it would be chiefly a matter of luck. In my opinion, he'd wait and then drive over to see how she made out. I can imagine him reaching the Moore garage and finding her asleep in the car, probably with the garage door open and the car motor turned off. All he'd have to do would be start the motor, close the garage door, and see Sheila was properly seated at the wheel. Then he'd leave, knowing the carbon monoxide would do his work."

Kim stared at him. "You make it sound so probable."

"It's only a theory," Derek said.

She frowned. "I think Dr. Taylor should tell the police about his suspicions. It isn't right that Jim Blake should get off scot-free. Helen did claim he was the father of her expected child."

Derek said, "You can rest easy on that score. Dr. Taylor decided to give all the information he had to the police as soon as Sheila was found dead."

"I'm so glad," she said with relief.

"I have an idea the police are quietly working on it now," he said.

191

She gave the museum director a troubled glance. "Of course Johnny has another theory."

"What is it?"

"He thinks Sheila shoved Helen overboard and then killed herself in remorse."

Derek Mills considered this. "I don't think so."

"Sheila *did* claim to see Helen's ghost," Kim reminded him. "And she was very upset about it."

"I'm still dubious about her guilt. I'd much sooner see Johnny himself as the murderer of both girls."

She nodded grimly. "I've thought of that also. I've seen him do so many weird things. How is Mack Carter?"

"His hand is coming around all right," Derek said, "no thanks to Johnny."

"He did that deliberately. There's a streak of madness in him!"

"Speaking of madness," Derek said glancing up at the second floor area of Craig House, "have you ever solved the mystery of the locked room? Do you still suspect that Johnny's Aunt Grace may be alive and hidden there?"

"I've not been bothered by any sounds from there lately," she admitted.

"So many other things have been happening," Derek said. "I saw you with that pleasant young man who sang with the orchestra the other night."

"Bill Griffith," she said. "He is a nice fellow, and he's worried about my being here."

"Will you stay on here now?" Derek asked.

"I think not," she said. "But I may wait a week or so to see if anything is discovered."

Derek Mills nodded. "You mean about Jim Blake and all that."

"Yes."

"Keep in touch with Dr. Taylor and me," Derek begged her. "We want to do all we can to protect you."

"Thank you," she said sincerely. And then they went back and joined the large group still standing talking and having drinks in the garden area.

Kim joined a circle of people listening to old Captain Zachary Miller. The old man gave her a smile of recognition as she came to stand near him. He was talking about the many shipwrecks near the island.

He said, "One of the worst was the wreck of the *British Queen*, bound from Dublin to America with two hundred and twenty-six Irish immigrants aboard. On a stormy night in December, after a couple of months at sea, she struck the shoals outside Dark Harbor. The poor immigrants packed in their narrow, cold, and filthy quarters below decks suffered every discomfort you can imagine as the ship pounded herself to pieces in the gale."

Dr. Taylor, who was in the circle, asked, "How many of them were saved?"

"All of them except two were saved," the ancient captain said. "A steamboat with two sloops in tow battled out to the stricken ship and carried out the rescue. One of the immigrants settled on the island and became a friend of mine. When the *British Queen* broke up, its name board floated in to shore. He found it and for years it could be seen over his barn door. His grandson is now the chief of police here."

"Chief Patrick Casey," Dr. Taylor said. "I talked with him only yesterday." And as he said this, he gave Kim a knowing look, meant to tell her that he had passed on his secret information about Jim Blake and Helen Walsh.

Kim understood because she had already been clued in by Derek. She asked, "Has Chief Casey held that job long?"

Captain Miller said, "About seven years. And before that

he was with the state police."

"Then he should be experienced," she said.

"He is," the old captain assured her.

The circle broke up and Kim and Dr. Taylor strolled on together to stand by the hedge which ran along three sides of the garden. He said, "You understood what I meant?"

"Yes, Derek had told me."

"Good," he said. "I feel better with the business off my chest. I only worry that I kept silent too long for Sheila's safety."

"I doubt that," she said. "What was Chief Casey's reaction?"

"I don't think he's much interested. He sees the happenings as normal accidents."

Distressed, she asked, "Does that mean he won't bother having any investigation?"

"I think he'll make a show of investigating," the doctor said. "But I doubt if he'll really work hard at it."

"That's discouraging."

"I may be doing him an injustice."

"I hope so," she said.

The late afternoon gathering came to an end. She went inside and came face to face with Jim Blake. The suave, mustached man gave her a bleak look.

"Glad to have that funeral over with," he said. "I think everyone is."

She studied him and thought he was extremely nervous. She said, "It was the last thing Sheila's friends could do for her."

"True," Jim said nervously.

"Were you and Sheila truly good friends?" she asked him.

He hesitated awkwardly. "We were friendly enough. She was always a rather difficult person to get along with. You ought to have known that!"

"I did," she said. "I thought I saw you buying her a drink at the dance."

He listened warily. "I may have. Your memory seems to be better than mine. I can't be sure that I did."

"I saw it," she said emphatically, although she'd made it up out of whole cloth. It was a stab in the dark in the hope of getting a vital target. By the young man's nervousness it had found a mark.

"Well, then I must have," he said. "I had no idea then that she'd be dead now."

"Didn't you?" she asked calmly and waited for his reaction.

It came quickly. Red suffused his good-looking but stern face and he demanded, "What sort of question was that?"

She was saved from answering by the appearance of Irma, who reminded him they had been invited to a dinner party on the other side of the island. Kim was relieved to see them go. She was close to being frightened by the sinister young lawyer.

Johnny's parents had gone off in their somber way and he had vanished somewhere. So, after a stroll in the garden, she went up to her room and shortly after that to bed. The ordeal of the day had also taken its toll on her. She felt jumpy and weary at the same time. The fog had vanished early that morning and it had remained fine all through the day. Now the stars could be seen reflecting on the dark water. The beam of Gull's Point Light cut through the sky.

She left the window and prepared for bed. By the time she turned the lights off she was ready to sleep. And sleep she did, though she had a bizarre nightmare about the funeral. She dreamt that Sheila rose from her coffin and denounced Jim Blake at her graveside!

Kim wakened with a start. She was perspiring and the dream she'd just had seemed very real to her. She knew it was nonsense and yet it was still vivid in her mind. She stared into the darkness and suddenly she heard a moan! And the moan came from that room which had been so long occupied by the madwoman! The room next to hers!

Fear shadowing her pretty face, she sat up in bed and waited until there was another groan from behind that locked door. She swung out of bed and crossed over to the door and pressed her ear against it. And she was certain she heard someone in there pacing restlessly up and down. Again she tried the doorknob and without any result.

She tried to make herself believe she had heard nothing. That her imagination had transformed creaking boards and some ordinary night sounds into moans and restless, pacing feet. So it was back to bed for her. This time sleep did not come as readily, but she did finally get a little rest.

By morning it was foggy again, and Johnny informed her it had been known to remain like that for a week. When she asked him where he'd gone the previous night, he mumbled something about having business in Dark Harbor. The real upset between them began when she told him of her dreams and then of hearing the sounds from the locked room.

Johnny had become angry. "The room is locked and empty. You heard nothing."

"You're wrong!" she protested.

"I don't think so," he said coldly. "It seems to me we have enough problems here without your adding more."

"I'm sorry," she said.

"You may well be," he replied and then strode away in a rage.

She followed him out hoping to reason with him but he got into his car and drove away. She watched the rear of the car vanish in the thick mist as she stood there in a mood of despair. There was nothing for it but to leave Craig House. Since the death of Sheila, the irate Johnny had become increasingly hard to get along with.

Turning, she strolled across the lawn to the path which led between the tall evergreens to the Moore property. She made her way along the lonely path and emerged on the other side. To her complete surprise, she saw Sheila's father standing on his own lawn.

The white-haired man looked as if someone had been keeping him neat. His suit was well-pressed and he had recently shaved. He showed surprise on seeing her.

"Miss Rice!" he exclaimed.

Not really understanding how she had come to wander so far, she said, "Hello, Mr. Moore. I must apologize. I didn't mean to trespass."

Archer Moore said, "No harm done. You're always welcome over here."

"Thank you," she said.

The big white-haired man showed sorrow on his ruined face. "These are proving difficult days for me."

"I'm sorry," she said.

Archer Moore gave her a solemn look. "You will recall I spoke to you about the phantom figure my daughter kept seeing?"

She nodded. "The ghost of Helen Walsh."

"Yes," he said. "Well, now I have seen her."

A chill ran down her spine as she stared at the big man. "Have you?"

"I have," he went on. He waved towards the house. "I heard something in the corridor and I went out and saw this soaking wet figure of a girl in an evening dress. I tell you it shocked me!"

"I can imagine!"

"I've heard sounds in the house nearly every night," he went on. "Why would Helen Walsh's ghost haunt my house?

What can be the meaning of it?"

She stood there in awkward silence. Then she said, "Some things are beyond understanding."

"Yes," he agreed. "That's true. Sheila said something like that. We talked about the ghost, but of course we got nowhere. And now I'm alone and bearing the grief of Sheila's loss and this ghost business."

"I hope it changes," she said.

"I hope so," the big man said. "You're staying on with the Craigs?"

"Just for a little."

"They're a cold lot," Archer Moore said bitterly. "That Johnny could have been a lot kinder to my daughter!"

"Johnny finds it hard to be kind to anyone."

The battered purple face of the big man twisted into an angry expression. "I remember once, when she was just a child, he tried to torment her. She was terrified of him. She claimed that he had caused the death of another youngster. I wouldn't listen to her."

"It will do you no good to brood on these things," she told him.

Archer Moore bowed his head. "I drink too much, you know."

"A lot of people do."

"I've been drinking heavily for years," the big man went on in a repentant tone. "If I hadn't been so drunk the night of the dance, I might have saved her."

She was afraid he would lead up to this. So she said, "I think we've discussed this before at the funeral home. You can't blame yourself. These things happen."

He stared at her. "You're not like the Craigs," he said. "You have a kind heart."

"Thank you."

He said, "About the matter Sheila mentioned before her death. I remembered it yesterday."

"Oh?"

"She told me if anything ever happened to her, to take care of her camera. It's a very good one, you know. Cost hundreds, and she prized it."

"Oh?" Kim was only casually interested but she tried to listen politely for the old man's benefit. He seemed so lonely and so much in need of someone to talk to.

"Yes," he went on. "The odd thing was that she suddenly stopped using it. For a time I didn't see the camera at all. And it was hidden away in a closet in her room. High up on a top shelf. My housekeeper found it when she was cleaning the place a bit."

"So you have it now?" she said.

"Yes," he replied. "And of course I will do as she asked. I will always keep it and treasure it. I have it locked in my desk. An odd request she made, wasn't it?"

"I don't think it so odd if she really valued the camera," Kim said. "She probably wanted to make you understand that it was something prized by her."

"Yes. I had been paying little attention to her and what she was doing," he agreed. He paused, then went on to say, "There are times when I'm not too responsible. Whole days go by in a fog. I lose touch completely. I was a failure as a husband and a bad father!"

"I think not," she said with a wan smile. "Sheila knew your failing, but she still loved you. I could tell that by the way she behaved when you were around. And she always spoke of you."

"She did care," Archer Moore said brokenly. "I know that. The lack of caring was on *my* part."

"Don't say that!" she protested, pained by his grief.

"You must come and visit me," the big man said. "Do come anytime. I need company. I'm very lonely."

"I will visit you," she promised.

He eyed her hopefully. "Would you like to come inside and have a drink with me now?"

"I'm afraid I haven't time," she excused herself. "But I will come back later."

"Do!" the big man urged as he stood there staring at her sadly.

She left him and retraced her steps along the path through the evergreens in a troubled state of mind. She hated to see the big man grieving as he was. If he kept on Johnny's prediction would undoubtedly come true. It would only be a short while until he had killed himself with his excessive drinking.

She had been touched by his story of Sheila's wanting him to treasure her camera if anything happened to her. And yet the story had its macabre side. Why should Sheila have dwelt so on death? Perhaps because of the Helen Walsh affair. Her drowning had preyed heavily on her mind. Could it have been because she had shoved the girl overboard? And had Sheila then begun to contemplate taking her own life? Eroded by guilt, had she begun to dwell on her death and the fate of her possessions afterwards? That seemed an explanation.

As she neared Craig House, Irma came out to the french doors by the garden and waved to her, calling out, "You have a phone call!"

"I'll be right there," Kim said, and began running towards the house.

Irma gave her a knowing look. "It's a young man—I think the fellow who came to the dance."

"Perhaps so," she said, and hurried on inside. She picked up the phone and was delighted to hear Bill's familiar voice over the line.

He said, "I read about Sheila Moore's death. It gave me a shock."

"We were all shocked," she told him.

"It sounded strange to me," he went on. "I'm more worried about you than ever!"

"I'll soon be leaving," she promised.

"I'm glad to hear it," the young stage manager said. "I can get you at least two weeks' work here before the end of the season. Can I tell the producer you're interested?"

"Yes," she said. "I'm planning to leave within a few days. I'll join you."

"That's the best news I've had," he said, relief clear in his voice. "Phone me just before you leave and I'll have a car meet you at the ferry."

"I'll do that," she promised.

"Just a parting word," Bill said, "I know now that I love you."

"We'll talk about that when we meet," she told him.

Their phone conversation ended on this note, and she went up to her room to do some preliminary packing. She was delighted to hear from Bill and she couldn't wait to join him. The island had lost its charm for her and so had Johnny Craig. With Sheila dead, there was no longer any excuse for her remaining to play the role of his fiancée! And she had no intention of taking on the part in real life. Johnny offered too much of a hazard. His cruel, neurotic streak terrified and sickened her.

She packed one of her bags with things she wouldn't be using every day. By the time she completed this task, it was close to the lunch hour. She went to the window to look out and saw that the fog had lifted a little. She also saw Johnny's car parked out front so she knew that he had returned and behind it there was another parked car with the word

"Police" on its door. This gave her a start! Derek Mills had suggested that the island's police chief would be calling around following up what Dr. Taylor had confided in him and it seemed he had lost no time doing it.

She went downstairs and discovered Johnny and Chief Pat Casey in a solemn conversation in the reception hall. When they saw her, they stopped talking.

Chief Casey gave her a nod of greeting. "How do you do, Miss Rice," he said.

"How do you do?" She returned his greeting.

The stout man told her, "I'm clearing up a few odds and ends. You knew Miss Moore fairly well, didn't you?"

"Sheila?" she said. "Yes. I came to know her. Why?"

Chief Casey's round face was serious. "You were at the dance on the night of her death?"

"Yes."

"Did she in any way suggest that she might be going to take her own life?"

She shook her head. "No. She was in very good spirits."

"I see," the chief said. "Thank you, Miss Rice. I may have a few questions to ask you later. Right now I must be on my way."

Johnny saw him out and then returned to her. He seemed in a chastened mood. The first thing he said was, "I'm sorry I was unpleasant to you this morning."

"It didn't matter," she said. And she felt it didn't since she had already decided to leave. "You don't need me here now that Sheila is dead."

Johnny looked troubled. "I may need you even more than I did before."

"I can't see that."

He sighed. "I can't understand why Chief Casey is suddenly going around asking questions. With Sheila's suicide, the Helen Walsh thing is closed. He should be willing to let it remain that way."

"I take it he isn't completely satisfied about the manner in which she met her death," Kim suggested.

"There was no big mystery about it," Johnny said darkly. "And for the record, that's how I feel."

"That's your privilege," she said quietly.

The handsome star was studying her rather nervously. He said, "I'm going to Falmouth today to see about the engagement there. I'll be back tomorrow and I hope I have some good word."

"I may take another job."

He showed surprise, then he asked, "With Bill Griffith?"

"Yes. I understand his company needs someone of my type for a couple of the final plays."

Johnny showed disgust. "It's only a small outfit without any big names. You'll be wasting your time!"

"I might like it."

"I'm almost sure I can get you into this big package show I'm planning to do," Johnny said. "Surely you'd prefer that?"

"Don't count on me!"

"I'm still try to get you the job. I'll know when I return tomorrow," he said.

Johnny left in the afternoon. It was another quiet day at Craig House. And at dinner that evening Irma announced that she was taking her parents to a concert in Dark Harbor. It was to be held in a private home there, and the wealthy sponsors had issued invitations.

"I'm sorry I can't ask you to accompany us," Irma lamented.

"Don't think about it," she protested. "I have some more packing to do. I'll be leaving tomorrow or the next day."

It was Irma's turn to register surprise. Her question was, "Does Johnny know?"

"Yes."

"Is he going to let you go?"

"Why not?"

"He's in love with you," Irma said. "I'm certain of it."

"I doubt that."

"He brought you here as his bride-to-be," Irma insisted.

"That's another story. Johnny will explain to you later."

Irma did not appear satisfied. She said, "I still say he won't let you go. Or if you do, he'll follow you. Is it that other fellow you're planning to meet?"

Kim said, "I have an offer to work with the playhouse where Bill is employed for the summer."

"But Johnny is going to appear at Falmouth. He said you would be in the play with him!"

"None of that is settled."

"I'm baffled," Irma said.

Kim felt she had no right to tell Johnny's sister more about their arrangement. But she would ask Johnny to explain when he returned. Shortly after dinner, Irma and her parents drove off to Dark Harbor, leaving Kim alone in the house except for the couple of servants who remained in the house at nights.

The fog had returned and was thicker than ever. The drone of the foghorn came along with the wash of the waves on the nearby shore. Kim wandered about the grim old mansion, too restless to settle down anywhere. She was standing in the library staring at the burning logs in the fireplace there when she heard a board creak by the doorway of the room.

Turning quickly she was startled to see Jim Blake standing there with a saturnine expression on his thin, mustached face. Uneasily, she said, "You came in almost without a sound."

"Did I frighten you?" he asked in a mocking tone.

She turned her back to the fireplace so that she was facing him. "Yes," she said. "But then this old house makes me terribly nervous."

"Why?"

She hesitated, feeling the possible murderer was playing a cat-and-mouse game with her. Then she managed, "I suppose Sheila's death has something to do with it. She used to be here a lot."

"There must be more than that," the suave young lawyer said.

"Things have happened here which I can't understand," she said. "I've heard strange sounds from that locked room upstairs, and I've seen things!"

"Such as?" Jim Blake had moved a step closer to her and there was an almost maniacal gleam in his eyes as he kept them fixed on her.

She tried to control the fear which had swept through her. She said, "I have seen the ghost of Helen Walsh—dripping from the ocean!"

Jim Blake's smile was coldly cynical. "Come now! I understood Sheila was the only one who saw that ghost."

"I have also seen it!" Her fears were overwhelming her so that there was a tremor in her voice.

"You didn't know Helen Walsh!" Jim Blake said, his voice harsh.

She swallowed nervously. "No. But she was a friend of yours, wasn't she?"

The young lawyer reacted to this. Looking a trifle shaken, he said, "She lived here on the island. I knew her. So did a lot of people."

"I understood you were especially friendly," she said.

Jim Blake stared at her. "Who told you that? Sheila?"

She felt that he was ready to attack her, silence her in any way he could and think about the consequences later. She knew she had to defend herself by making him somehow afraid.

So she said, "Not Sheila! Dr. Taylor told me she spoke to him about you!"

Jim Blake gasped. "I don't believe it."

"It's true," she said. "And I think that Dr. Taylor mentioned it to Chief Casey. He was here talking to the Craigs today. I think he's not satisfied with the accidents which took Helen's and Sheila's lives."

Her revelations had the desired effect. Jim Blake lost all his menace and he questioned her in a shaky voice, "You're not lying to me?"

"Everything I've said is the truth," she told him. "Why should you be so concerned?"

"I'm not concerned," he said without conviction. Then he asked, "What time do you expect Irma and her parents back?"

"About eleven, I think."

"I'll wait for them," Jim Blake said. "I want to talk to Irma." And he turned abruptly and left the library and walked up the hallway to the living room.

She guessed that he would make himself some drinks and prepare some sort of story for Irma when she returned. He had reacted so strongly to her mention of Helen and Dr. Taylor that she was almost convinced he was guilty of shoving Helen overboard and then of committing another murder to silence Sheila. And now he must be worrying that he'd not save himself, but merely placed a rope around his neck.

The prospect of being in the old house with him for the next two hours was not appealing. She hesitated in the library wondering what to do. Then she recalled that she had an open invitation to visit Archer Moore next door whenever she liked. This could be an ideal solution to her problem.

She furtively made her way from the library and then out the side french doors. In a moment she was crossing the lawn to the evergreens and the path which led to the Moore mansion. The air was damp and chilly. The gray mist still mantled everything. She shivered as much from fear as from the fog. She hoped that Jim had not seen her leave and that he wasn't following her.

Finally she reached the door of the Moore house. She rang the bell and after a few minutes the door was opened by a stern-looking woman who proved to be the housekeeper. She showed Kim in to the study where a dressing-gowned Archer Moore sat in a large leather easy chair with a glass of some sort of liquor in his hand.

His wrecked purple face took on a smile and he rose to greet her rather unsteadily. "Delighted to see you, Miss Rice," he said. "I would have dressed if I'd known you were coming."

"That doesn't matter," she said. "I'm sorry to intrude. But I was alone and I thought it might be pleasant to come over here for a little."

"You are most welcome," Sheila's father said. "Let me fix you a drink."

"A weak one," she told him.

He prepared her drink as she took in the softly lighted, book-lined room. It had great elegance about it. Prominent in its decorations was a fine oil portrait of Sheila which smiled down from above the fireplace.

Archer Moore came back with her drink and gave it to her. He noticed that she was admiring the painting. "It's like she was, isn't it?" he said.

"Yes," she agreed.

"I get great comfort from it," he said. And then with a

change of thought, he went on, "I told you about the camera she valued so much."

"Yes."

"I've made a decision about it. I'm not going to merely keep it locked up forever. I want it used and enjoyed. So I'm giving it to you."

"Oh, no!" she protested. "You want it as a keepsake."

"I have many others," Archer Moore told her. "No, you shall have the camera." And he crossed to his desk, took some keys from his pocket, selected one and rather shakily unlocked the desk drawer and removed a small camera from it. "It's not large," he said, turning to offer it to her.

"It's one of the new vest-pocket size," she agreed. "I still think you should keep it."

"It's yours," the big man said, pressing it on her.

As he turned to lock the desk drawer again she began to examine the tiny camera which was only about four inches long and an inch thick and wide. It was while she was examining it that she discovered that it was still loaded with film. Only four snapshots had been taken. And a sudden excitement shot through her as she wondered what it was that Sheila had been so zealously protecting—the camera or the film in it?

CHAPTER TWELVE

The evening went by and Archer Moore continued drinking, gradually becoming more maudlin. Kim was embarrassed, but she did not want to leave and return to Craig House to be alone with Jim Blake. As the white-haired man seated opposite her in the leather chair rambled on, sometimes incoherently, she kept an eye on her wristwatch and bided her time to leave.

She had carefully placed the camera in a pocket of her raincoat. The knowledge that there was film in it had excited her, and she could hardly wait to place it in the hands of Derek Mills, whom she was certain she could trust. It was her thought that what Sheila had been guarding so carefully was the film, rather than the camera. Derek could have the film developed and then they would know.

Archer Moore broke in her thoughts by saying, "Sheila always intended to marry Johnny Craig! It didn't matter how badly he behaved toward her, she always remained in love with him!"

"That sometimes happens," she said.

The white-haired man eyed her drunkenly. "Even when he brought you here and said you and he were to be married, my Sheila still didn't lose hope."

"I know."

"Johnny's no good," the old man said. "No good for Sheila or for you!" His words slurred badly as he finished and his head bent forward. The glass dropped from his hand. He was deep in sleep.

With some embarrassment she got up and picked up the

glass from the floor and placed it on the table beside him. He was breathing heavily and unaware of anything going on around him. Next she went to the kitchen and told the housekeeper. The stern-faced woman did not seem at all surprised that her employer had passed out from drinking. It appeared to be a regular occurrence.

Kim said good night and started back to Craig House. She lingered a moment on the steps to button her raincoat all the way to the neck. The fog was still thick and it was cold. Then she resolutely started across the wet lawn towards the path which led through the evergreens. It had been a strange, macabre sort of night.

As a result she was in a definitely nervous state. As she neared the tall trees their branches reached out of the mist like black, menacing arms. She shrank from the lonely passage along the tree-lined path, but there was no turning back. She had gone only a few steps through the wooded area when she was filled with a terrifying feeling that she was being followed.

It came to her in a flash that she could not shake off. She increased her pace and prayed that she was wrong. But within a few seconds, she heard the sounds of footsteps close behind her! With a frightened sob she glanced over her shoulder and saw the phantom!

Close on her heels came the ghostly figure of the drowned Helen Walsh! Kim cried out in horror and began to run! This proved a fatal error for the path was uneven and crooked. Almost at once she stumbled and fell. As she did so, the phantom figure pounced on her and she felt icy fingers clenching her throat!

In the darkness and terror, she could not make out anything about her assailant clearly. She fought as hard as she could to escape the phantom, and after a short struggle managed to free herself. With a pounding heart she got to her feet and ran for freedom once again. And she could hear the phantom close behind her!

Somehow she raced along without stumbling for a second time. At last she was in the open and crossing the lawn. But the phantom was close to her again. She felt a hand clutch her by the arm and whirl her around. She fell to the ground with the phantom once again trying to throttle her. She screamed for help hoping someone in the Craig mansion might hear her! But she feared it would do no good! And gradually the steely hands of the phantom were closing off her breathing.

When she finally gave up the struggle and lay back, she was conscious of a bright light filling the darkness. It seemed that this might be a herald of death. The hands seemed to release her throat and there was no more struggle. Accompanying the light there were voices and she wondered vaguely what this might mean.

Someone shook her and she found herself gazing up into the round face of Chief of Police Pat Casey. The chief was bending down with a concerned expression as he inquired, "What happened to you?"

"I came through the woods," she sobbed. "And she came after me!"

"*She?*" the police chief echoed in surprise.

Kim was up on an elbow now. "Yes," she said. "Only your coming along saved me. Your headlights bore down on us at just the proper moment to rescue me!"

"If what you say is true, you're right," the chief said. "Are you able to stand?"

"Yes," she said, struggling to her feet with the help of the chief. She straightened out her rumpled raincoat and felt that the camera was still resting in its left pocket.

Now that the terror was over, she began to feel some embarrassment. She said, "Thank you."

He was staring at her with a suspicious air. "I drove down here on a routine check," he said. "I often do this. I heard your screams above the sound of the car engine. Then the beam of my headlights caught you on the ground. But I saw no one else!"

"There was the ghost!"

Chief Casey gave her a tolerant look. "Ghosts aren't quite in my line, Miss Rice. You say that someone followed you and attacked you?"

"Yes!"

"What did your attacker look like?"

"I saw her only once," she said unhappily. "And she was dressed in a sequined black dress and there was seaweed draped on her face and shoulders. It was the ghost of Helen Walsh!"

The chief eyed her silently for a moment before he said, "It seemed to you like the ghost of Helen Walsh?"

"Yes!"

The chief sighed. "Either someone made themselves up that way to terrify you, or you had only a blurred impression of the person and filled in some of the details yourself."

"I didn't imagine it!" she protested.

"I didn't say that you did," the chief said. "You are all right?"

"Yes."

"Then I'll see you safely into the house and take a look around. Whoever it was can't have gotten far away."

"Unless it was a ghost," she said.

"In which case I can't be of any assistance to you," the chief said stolidly.

He escorted her to the door of Craig House and told her he would come back and report to her after a little. Still exhausted and fearful from her ordeal, she went inside. The house was all in silence and she realized that she had stayed longer at Archer Moore's than she'd intended. It had been difficult to break away until he passed out. Now it was past midnight.

She waited in the reception hall and saw Chief Casey put out his car lights and then begin to make a search of the area on foot with a large flashlight to search out the dark places. She saw him go along the path to the Moore estate and vanish.

"What are you doing down there in the darkness?" a voice demanded, taking her by surprise.

Kim wheeled around to see Madeline Craig in a robe and nightgown standing midway down the broad stairs. The older woman had a look of annoyance on her thin face.

Kim said, "I've been visiting Mr. Moore. On the way back, I was chased by someone. Chief Casey came along and my attacker fled. He is out there now looking for whoever it was."

Madeline Craig lifted her eyebrows and in an icy tone, said, "I have never known anything like that to happen here before."

"I can't help that," she said. "I'm telling you the truth. Did Irma see Jim Blake when she came home?"

"There was no one here when we returned," Johnny's mother said. "No one at all. We went straight up to bed."

"He was here earlier. He wanted to see Irma," she said.

"I expect he had manners enough to leave when it became so late," Madeline Craig said. "I cannot stand here talking all night. As nothing serious has happened, I'll return to bed." And she did.

More let down than ever, Kim returned to waiting for the chief to come back. After what seemed an endless wait he did come. She saw the glow of his flashlight through the mist as he came slowly towards the front door. She went out on the steps to greet him.

"Did you find anyone?" she asked.

"I'm sorry, Miss," the chief said. "I didn't."

She sighed. "I'm not surprised."

"Best that you go to bed and try to forget it," the chief advised her. "I'll keep an eye out for anyone as I drive back to the main road."

"Thanks," she said wearily.

"And don't venture out at night alone in the future," was his advice.

"I won't," she promised. "I'm sorry to have been such a bother!"

"Part of my duties, Miss," the chief said. And with that he tipped his cap to her and went back toward his car.

It was a dismal ending to a completely grim night. Kim made her way up to her room in a shattered state. There was no doubt in her mind she'd seen the ghost, even though it was unlikely anyone would believe her. Then she felt the camera in her pocket and this heartened her. She felt she might have made some slight progress. She would know as soon as she contacted Derek Mills and had him develop the film.

That night she slept badly again. In her nightmares she relived the terrifying moment in the woods when the phantom had attacked her. She twisted and moaned beneath the sheets just as she had under the torment of those icy hands! At last it was morning.

Irma was at the breakfast table to greet her. The attractive girl said, "Mother tells me Jim Blake was here last night."

Kim sat opposite her. "Yes. He intended to wait until you came home."

"He didn't."

"I gathered that," she said.

Irma showed some uneasiness. "Did he say what he wanted to see me about?"

"No."

"Strange that he left," Irma said. "And you weren't here all evening?"

"No. I went over to visit with Archer Moore."

Irma showed surprise. "Really?"

"Yes. I thought I should. He's so lonely."

"He was drunk, of course," Irma said with disgust.

"I'm afraid he was."

"I don't know how you could stand to spend a whole evening with him."

"I feel sorry for him."

"Sheila hated you."

Kim considered, "I wouldn't say that. I think she was annoyed at my appearance on the scene. But I doubt if she really hated anyone."

Irma's eyebrows raised. "How can you be such an authority on her? You didn't know her all that well."

"I think I knew her well enough," she said.

"I'm amazed," was Irma's reply. She touched her napkin to her lips and got up from the table. "I must try and get in touch with Jim and see what he wanted," she said. And she went out.

At this time all Kim could think about was that film. As soon as she finished breakfast she borrowed the station wagon with a reluctant sort of permission from Stephen Craig. Johnny's father told her, "It's really Johnny's personal car, but I guess he won't mind you driving it."

"He's let me have it before," she assured the dour, elder Craig.

He shrugged. "Well, go ahead then."

She knew she would be glad to escape from the gloomy old

mansion with its frigid people. She drove straight across the island to the museum on the hill, skirting around the main part of the town of Dark Harbor. As soon as she reached the museum she went inside and up to Derek Mills's office.

The handsome director of the museum was standing just by the doorway of his office in conversation with Captain Zachary Miller. Both men gave their attention to her, seeming glad to see her.

She was breathless from running up the stairs. "I hope I'm not interrupting anything!" she gasped.

Captain Miller chuckled and said, "Nothing more serious than the subject of my lecture tomorrow. You've got nice red cheeks this morning."

"From rushing, I suppose," she smiled weakly.

Derek Mills looked interested. "You've something to see me about?"

"Yes," she said.

The old captain said, "I'll be on my way."

Derek Mills stopped him by touching his arm. "No," he said. "I think it might be good to have you here. Do you agree, Kim?"

"I have no objections," she said.

"Let's go inside," Derek Mills suggested.

Kim quickly told the two men about Jim Blake calling at the house when she was alone and the oddness of his behavior. She also pointed out that he had seemed frightened when she'd mentioned Helen and Dr. Taylor.

She apologized, "Maybe I shouldn't have, but I was desperate to protect myself. I hoped it might upset him, and it did."

"No harm done," Derek said. "He is bound to find out about it soon. You didn't mention that Helen named him as the one responsible for her pregnancy?"

"I didn't tell him that, but I'm sure he guessed it. I say that because of the way he reacted."

"I'm not surprised," Derek said.

"Then I went over to Archer Moore's to get away from Blake," she said. And she went on to tell them about the camera and the film in it. She ended by passing the camera to Derek Mills.

He studied it grimly. "This may hold the answer we've been looking for."

Captain Miller said, "If it has a snapshot of Jim Blake shoving Helen overboard, it will save the chief a lot of trouble."

"I was thinking the same thing," Derek Mills agreed. He told Kim, "I have an assistant who develops film in a darkroom we have here. He's out for lunch. As soon as he comes back, I'll have him develop the film."

"I can hardly wait," she said.

"No wonder you arrived so excited," Captain Miller said.

She remained to talk with the two for a few minutes longer. Derek promised her he'd let Dr. Taylor know what had gone on. He also said he would phone her as soon as the film was developed and let her know what was on it. As she drove back to Craig House, she began to have qualms. Suppose the film turned out to have nothing of value on it? The print might be something very ordinary or perhaps blurred so that nothing could be identified from it!

The fog had drifted seaward again, and the sun was shining when she reached the old mansion. She decided that she would take a dip in the pool before lunch. Anything to keep her occupied until she heard the results of the film developing. She went upstairs to her room and was making her way down the dark hallway when she saw a door open and the gaunt figure of Madeline Craig emerge into the corridor. And she gasped because she knew that Johnny's mother had just come out of the locked room—the room in which mad Aunt Grace had been kept!

Now she saw the gaunt woman carefully locking the door after her. And then she came down the corridor toward Kim. It was inevitable that they would have to pass and greet each other.

Kim spoke first, saying, "I don't often see you up here, Mrs. Craig."

The gaunt face of the older woman had a guilty expression. She said impassively, "I sometimes check the various rooms to make sure that everything is as it should be."

"I see," she said.

There was no further exchange as Madeline Craig marched on in her usual arrogant fashion. Kim was intrigued to know that the older woman had visited the room and felt there was a reason beyond the one offered.

Kim thought about this as she changed into her bathing suit. She hardly believed that the mad old Grace was still alive and in that room. But there was some macabre secret about it which the Craigs were determined she shouldn't find out. Several times she felt she'd been near discovering the truth about it, but always she'd been disappointed. Even Johnny had shown anger at her interest in the room.

She went down to the pool and spent a half-hour in the water. She took a shower in the pool cabana and then put on her dressing gown over her suit to return to the house. She was on her way upstairs when the phone in the hall rang. Irma came out of the living room to answer it. After a moment she looked up and said, "Wait! It's for you! Johnny!"

"Oh," she said. And she hurried back down. Johnny was in Falmouth seeing about doing the Neil Simon play there. Perhaps he was phoning her that the engagement had been arranged.

She took the phone and said, "How did you make out, Johnny?"

"I'm going to do the show," he told her. "And they can use you."

"I think not," she said, glancing to see if Irma was still in the hallway and relieved to see that she had gone off somewhere.

"We'll talk about it when I get back," Johnny said. "What has been happening while I've been gone?"

"Plenty," she said. "I saw the ghost again."

"Spare me that!" he pleaded.

"It's true. And something else. I was given a camera by Archer Moore. Sheila's camera—and it has film in it."

Johnny at once reacted. "Do you have it there?"

"No. I've given it to Derek Mills," she said.

"To Mills?" he exclaimed. "Why?"

"I hardly dare tell you on the phone," she said tensely. "It may be that the film will show who killed Helen Walsh. I have an idea Sheila took a snapshot of the murder that night."

There was a brief silence for a moment. Then he said, "You are talking wildly."

"Derek thinks the film may show the murderer. It isn't all that wild. Sheila kept the camera hidden away."

"You always come up with something new," Johnny said in a grim voice. "We'll discuss it when I get back."

"When will that be?"

"I'll come on the late afternoon ferry," he said. "Just one more thing. If Sheila took the snapshot, who does Derek Mills think the murderer was?"

"Jim," she said in a low tone that was almost a whisper.

From the other end of the line, Johnny sounded shocked, "Irma's Jim?"

"Yes."

"Preposterous," Johnny said. "I'll see you soon."

"Yes," she said. "We'll know by the time you're back. There may not be anything important on the film, or it may have been ruined."

"I'll be interested in hearing about it when I get there," Johnny said. "Have you missed me?"

"Of course."

"Does that mean you've changed in your attitude toward me?"

She avoided answering. "That's something else we can discuss when we meet again."

She went upstairs and then came down to join the others for lunch. Stephen and Madeline Craig argued all through the meal about some household hills which had been mislaid. And Irma was pale-looking and strangely silent. It struck Kim that the other girl might have listened in to her conversation with Johnny on one of the extension phones. In that case it was easy to understand why she was upset. She would have heard that Jim Blake was the one under suspicion.

As they left the table Kim asked Irma, "Did you get in touch with Jim to find out about last night?"

Irma flashed her an annoyed look. "No," she said. "Jim is on the mainland for a day or two. He left this morning."

This was news! Had Jim left the island because he knew he was suspected of Helen's murder? Kim knew she had given him enough clues to let him deduce this during their talk. It began to look as if the guilty man might have made his escape.

Kim pretended to take the information in a casual way and said, "Well, you'll see him when he comes back."

"I suppose so," Irma said bleakly and she went upstairs, leaving Kim alone in the hall.

Kim read a magazine in the living room as she remained

near the phone waiting for the all-important call from Derek Mills. As time for the call drew near she became more and more upset. She was so nervous she could only turn the pages of the magazine and pretend to be reading.

Around two-thirty she heard a car drive up. She rose and looked out the bay windows to see Derek Mills in the car. She put down the magazine and rushed outside to greet him.

One look at Derek's handsome face as she crossed the gravel walk to greet him told her there was something dreadfully wrong. She said, "I've been waiting for your call."

The young museum director nodded. "I knew you would be. But I decided I had better come personally."

She stared at him. "What about the film?"

"It's developed."

"Did it turn out?"

He nodded again. "Yes."

"And does it show the murderer?"

"It does," Derek said in a taut voice.

"Who?"

He hesitated. Then, in a grim voice, he told her. "Johnny!"

She raised her hands to the side of her face. "Johnny!"

"Yes," he glanced uneasily towards the house. "That is why I felt I had to come myself and tell you."

Tears filled her eyes and she kept a hand pressed to one of her temples. "I have always feared it might be Johnny, but I began to suspect Jim Blake."

"Don't break down!" Derek pleaded with her. "We have to play this carefully."

"Does Chief Casey know?"

"Yes," Derek Mills said. "And so does Dr. Taylor. By the way, he had the chief do some investigating, and it turns out that Helen Walsh lied to the doctor."

"About what?"

"About where she was when she went to the mainland. She didn't meet Jim Blake in Boston. She was registered at a motel in Hyannis on that date, and Johnny Craig had an adjoining room."

Kim's eyes widened. "So it was Johnny who was responsible for her pregnancy, not Jim."

"That seems to be it," Derek Mills said grimly.

"And Sheila cared enough about him to still try to blackmail him into marriage with that film. She told him she had it, and that was why she was so certain he wouldn't dare not marry her."

"So he put sleeping pills in her drink the night of the dance and then went back and arranged that suicide scene. But he only got rid of her. He didn't get the film," Derek pointed out.

She gave the museum director a horrified look. "I told him about it."

"About what?"

"The film!"

"When?"

"He called here about two hours ago," she said. "I told him you had the film and everything. I said we suspected Jim."

Derek whistled under his breath. "That about does it! What did he say?"

"He seemed upset!"

"I can bet that," he said grimly.

"He'll know!" she said.

"When is he due back?" Derek wanted to know.

"He said late this afternoon."

"And he's at Falmouth?"

"Yes."

Derek said, "I'll have to let Chief Casey know."

"You can phone him from here," she said.

"No," he said. "I don't want to tell the Craigs yet. I'll drive to the police station in Dark Harbor."

Kim was in a panic. "When will you tell the Craigs?"

Derek sighed. "I'll ask the chief. Maybe I'll come back here after I see him and tell them what we've found out so far."

"Can I go to Dark Harbor with you and then drive back here when you return?" she begged him. "I can't face them now. They'll ask a lot of questions about your being here."

"All right," Derek said. "Hurry!" And he opened the car door for her.

The next two hours were like something lifted from a delirium. She heard the grim discussion at police headquarters and then when Chief Casey tried to locate Johnny in Falmouth, they found out he'd left there at noon. No one knew where he had gone.

Chief Casey put down the phone with a sigh and told them, "I'm afraid Miss Rice told Johnny too much. He's on the run now!"

"How far can he go?" Derek asked.

"Not far," the chief told him. "I'll send out an alarm and then have it relayed to all the adjoining states. We have the license number and make of the car he's driving. It is the property of the theater."

When this was settled, they left the police station and drove back to Craig House. There Derek assembled the family and told them that Johnny was in deep trouble. The reactions of the three were what might have been expected.

Irma burst into tears and ran upstairs after sobbing, "I don't believe it!"

Madeline Craig rose and said stiffly, "If you will excuse me, I must look after my daughter." And she also left.

The aristocratic and arrogant Stephen Craig frowned and said, "I expect you'll find that murder photo a fake. That Sheila was a vixen, capable of anything."

Derek and Kim then drove over to Archer Moore's and found the big white-haired man comparatively sober. He listened to what they had to say with a grave expression on his blotched purple face. Then he said, "So it is all too likely that Johnny murdered my Sheila?"

"I'm afraid so," Derek said.

"I'm not surprised," Archer Moore said. "Not at all. There is madness in the Craig family."

"You're thinking of his Aunt Grace," Derek said.

"And long before that," the big man told them. "The history of this island and the Craigs who have lived here will tell you. One in every generation seemed to be cursed with the streak of insanity."

Derek said, "He's taken a car from the Falmouth Playhouse and driven off somewhere."

"Sheila would be worrying about him if she were here," the big man said with a hint of tenderness in his voice. "She loved him though she knew he was a murderer."

"Evidently," Derek agreed.

"But what about the ghost?" Archer Moore wanted to know. "What about the ghost of Helen Walsh?"

"Yes," Kim said, turning to Derek. "I'd like to know about the ghost, too."

Derek gave her a solemn look. "I have an idea if you spend another night in Craig House, you'll see the ghost again."

"What do you mean?" she asked.

"I'll tell you," he said. And he proceeded to explain it all in detail.

So Kim decided to spend one last night at Craig House. Then she planned to hurry to the mainland and join Bill at the

Cape Playhouse. She knew she could never bring herself to tell Johnny's family the truth about her coming to Dark Harbor. Even if she did tell them that Johnny had hired her to play the role of his fiancée, she was sure they wouldn't believe her.

They were grieving in their own silent way, waiting for word about Johnny. By late evening the police had still not found him. Since the Craigs deliberately avoided her, she went up to bed early and finished all but the very last of her packing. Then she went to bed.

It was a lovely moonlit night in contrast to the brooding fog which had gone before. She was still stunned by the revelations of the day—so much so that she was in a state of numbness rather than of fear. Sleep was difficult. But at last her eyes closed in weariness.

When she opened them again it was with a start! For standing at the foot of her bed in the gleaming moonlight was the ghost of Helen Walsh! There was no question of it! The ghost wore the familiar sequined black dress and seaweed was draped on her hair and on her face. But this time there was a difference—this time the ghost held a long, gleaming knife in her hand!

Kim screamed! And as she did the ghost of the drowned girl rushed at her with the knife. At the same instant a figure sprang out from a closet beside the bed. It was Derek Mills, who had hidden himself there and now came to struggle with the phantom!

It was the phantom's turn to scream wildly! Kim turned on the room lights as Derek wrested the knife from the sobbing ghost! He then pulled back the draped hair from her face to reveal the hate-distorted features of Irma Craig!

"I meant to kill you!" Irma cried out at her as she struggled in Derek's arm.

Dr. Taylor came and administered a heavy sedative to the

hysterical girl. When she was safely in bed, the elderly doctor informed her shocked parents that Irma would undoubtedly have to be placed in a sanitarium for a while to restore her to full mental health.

"It is the best way out," the old doctor counseled them. "I fear that otherwise she will face serious criminal charges."

At last humble, Stephen Craig placed a comforting arm around his wife and told the doctor, "I leave it entirely in your hands, Dr. Taylor."

The next morning Derek came and picked her up and took her to the ferry at Dark Harbor. When she arrived there, she was pleasantly surprised to discover both Captain Miller and Dr. Taylor there. They had come to see her on her way.

Captain Miller told her, "I should have remembered long ago that Irma isn't really a Craig. She was adopted when she was a baby. I remember it well. I guess I forgot it because it didn't seem important."

"It *was* important," Dr. Taylor said dryly. "She was in love with Johnny and playing her own game to keep him for herself all the time. That's why she tormented Sheila as Helen's ghost, and also Kim. There was no romance between Jim and her. That was a pretense on her part."

Derek said, "And Jim nearly wound up being accused of Helen's murder."

"No danger of that now," Dr. Taylor said.

"So Irma isn't really a Craig at all," she said. "Yet she has surely suffered some sort of mental breakdown."

Dr. Taylor shrugged. "Too close association with the Craigs, and especially Johnny. I guarantee those two were closer than most of us guessed."

The ferry whistle blew as a warning for tardy passengers to get aboard. Kim turned to the three men who had befriended her. "I don't know how to thank you."

Captain Miller chuckled. "Do that by coming back to see us one day."

"I will," she promised.

Dr. Taylor smiled at her in his friendly way. "Thank Derek. He is the one who did the most for you."

"I know," she said. And turning to him, she said, "I do thank you, Derek. And I hope we meet again."

He nodded. "So do I," he said. "In happier circumstances."

Then she hurried aboard the ferry. Derek had already seen to her baggage. She stayed on the rear deck for several minutes waving to them. And gradually the wharf and Dark Harbor faded in the distance and she could not make them out any longer. The ferry went out of the harbor and she had a final glimpse of the island.

Bill Griffith was at the dock at Woods Hole to greet her. He kissed her and helped her into the car he'd brought. Only when they were ready to leave did he show her the afternoon paper and the story with large black headlines, "Noted Actor Dies in Car Crash!" She didn't need to read the rest. Her eyes blurred with tears.

He took the paper from her. "The end of Johnny," he said.

"Yes," she said. "So much talent lost. I wonder what he would have been like if only he hadn't had that streak of madness." And she knew that in her heart it was something she would always wonder about.